THE BLACK-EYED KIDS

RANDOLPH CASEY HORROR THRILLERS
BOOK 3

ROCKWELL SCOTT

THE BLACK-EYED KIDS

PROLOGUE

Somethin' ain't right.

Wayne Swanson peered out the window of his front door, studying his vast yard as best he could in the pitch-black night. There were no streetlights in the rural area where he lived, so the only light came from the moon. Wind whipped at the trees, blowing the dead brown leaves all over his lawn. Old Pat on the news channel had said the wind speeds were low, but to Wayne's eyes it looked like a hurricane was coming. He'd endured plenty of those in his long life.

He sipped his whiskey, savoring the burn in his mouth and the back of his throat. He didn't drink often, but that night he needed to calm his nerves.

"It's the weather, Wayne," his wife Geraldine said behind him. "The weather guys can't predict it no matter how much they try, and neither can you. Stop obsessing."

It wasn't the weather that bothered him, though. He was on the lookout for something else. Twice in the past

I

week he'd had trespassers on his property, and they'd come around the same time both nights.

"The weather ain't the problem, Gerry," Wayne said, never taking his eyes from the window.

His wife sighed. "Honestly, Wayne. You can't call the police *again*."

Wayne pressed his lips together. He'd called the police after both occurrences, but they'd turned up nothing. The second time, the officer had given Wayne that look he'd come to recognize. The one that seemed to say, "just another old-timer losing it." Not even Geraldine believed he'd seen anyone.

Boss, Wayne's bullmastiff, whined and scratched at the back door, wanting to go out. Wayne checked his watch. It was 9:49 PM. Close to the time the trespassers had come the last two times.

Wayne downed the rest of his whiskey in a single gulp and went to the kitchen. Boss looked over his shoulder at Wayne, eyes big and pleading.

"Yeah, yeah." Wayne placed his empty glass on the nearby counter and crouched down to lace up his boots. Even at eighty-one, he could still bend, sit, and work. He was blessed. Sadly, his wife couldn't say the same.

"Are you taking the dog out?" Geraldine's voice came from the living room.

"Yup," Wayne said. He finished tightening his boots and straightened up.

Geraldine appeared in the kitchen. Her long, white hair was tied up in a loose bun and she wore her white night gown, ready for bed. "Try to keep him calm. He'll wake the neighbors."

"We ain't got neighbors," Wayne said, annoyed at how

often he had to remind her. The residents of Plaster Road, the Swansons included, owned large plots of land. Their nearest neighbor on one side was about a mile away. On the other side, two miles away. There had once been a closer house, but it had been demolished, leaving behind a vast, unused portion of land. Wayne wondered when the owner—whoever it was—was going to build something there.

Wayne opened the closet next to the back door. His shotgun leaned against the wall. He grabbed it and checked to make sure it was loaded. It was.

"Wayne." Geraldine's hand went to her collarbone. "What in God's name?"

"Somethin' ain't right, Geraldine." He grabbed the flashlight off the closet shelf, checked that it worked, and opened the back door. Boss bolted outside.

Wayne knew Geraldine didn't like his gun. Knew she didn't believe that he'd seen anyone on their property. The police had failed him twice, so if these goons were going to keep harassing him, he would have to take matters into his own hands. Wayne Swanson did not like to take chances if he could avoid it.

Forty years ago, burglars had broken into their home and made off with a bunch of stuff. The most valuable had been some of Geraldine's family jewelry. His wife had cried for days after losing things with such sentimental value. Wayne had sympathized with her, but he always knew it could have ended up so much worse. What if they'd come home during the burglary? And if they had, what if those criminals had been armed?

The nighttime walk around the house had been a ritual ever since Boss was a pup. Wayne called it "the patrol." Boss couldn't, and wouldn't, settle down to sleep until he sniffed around the perimeter of the house, circling the entire property and scoping everything out. He would pee here and there, drink a bit from his outdoor water bowl, and when they returned inside he'd curl up on his cushion in the corner and snore until dawn. Innocent enough, at least until recently, when the patrol had become a lot more sinister.

That's what had frightened Wayne the most. Both times, the trespassers had come during the nightly walk, as if they knew Wayne would be outside. If they knew his routine, that meant they'd been lurking around for a lot longer than a week.

The wind whistled past Wayne's ears and whipped at his shirt. It was unusually cold for autumn in the south, and the chill pierced through the thin cotton material. He trained the flashlight's beam onto the ground in front of him. Boss dipped in and out of the light, sniffing around and leading the way. Wayne's boots crunched through piles of dead leaves so thick that they bunched around his ankles. He'd have to rake them in the morning before they rose to the roof.

The roof. That means the gutter's gonna be full, too. He didn't mind cleaning those out, but it was always a pain because Geraldine didn't like it when he climbed the ladder. She would no doubt shout at him all day, telling him to come down and pay someone to do that before he fell and broke his neck.

Wayne and Boss circled the house and came to the empty lot next door, the one where the abandoned house had been demolished by the new owner. Boss never wandered too far onto it, as if he knew the property line.

He sniffed the ground and looked around, then paused with one leg up, poised to pee.

Suddenly, Boss's entire body stiffened. He started growling.

Wayne pointed his flashlight toward where his dog was looking. The beam illuminated only an empty field.

"Who's there?" he shouted. Wayne tightened his grip on his shotgun.

Boss backed up against Wayne's ankles. The dog was usually fearsome and wanted nothing more than to tear the mailman apart, and no visitor had ever scared him. But whatever Boss sensed in the empty lot next door turned him into a cowering mess.

"T-this is trespassing," Wayne shouted. "I'll c-call the police."

No response.

Wayne's flashlight blinked out like an extinguished torch, plunging him and Boss into darkness. Wayne mashed the button several times, thinking he'd pressed it by accident, but it didn't come back on.

"What the hell?" he muttered. He'd just changed the damn batteries.

Boss let out a single, aggressive bark. Wayne dropped his useless flashlight and gripped his shotgun in both hands.

Then, even though it was dark, Wayne saw them. The two familiar black shadows stood in the middle of the empty lot, side-by-side, one taller than the other.

Wayne raised his shotgun and pointed it straight at the pair. "I've got a gun. You'd better leave." His aim was unsteady in his trembling hand.

They remained completely still, like statues.

Wayne Swanson wasn't seeing things. He was eighty-one years old, but Dr. Hays praised his eyesight every year when he went in for his checkup. Yet how could those shadows be there in the first place? It made no sense. You had to have light to make shadows. It was like the shadows were darker than the night.

Wayne pumped the shotgun, hoping the sound would frighten the trespassers. "I'm warnin' you. This is private property."

Boss started whimpering and crying.

Wayne considered firing a warning shot. Far up and to the left, of course, only to scare the bastards off. But if he did shoot, he'd never hear the end of it from Geraldine, who'd likely think he was only firing at figments of his imagination.

A sharp gust of wind almost knocked Wayne off his feet. It was like something from a storm, though Old Pat hadn't said anything about a storm coming in. The leaves whipped around Wayne, lifted from the ground, and were carried up like a mass migration of birds, breaking his line of sight on the trespassers.

Boss relaxed. When the leaves settled, Wayne saw that he and Boss were alone. The intruders had run away again.

Wayne scooped up his flashlight, pressed the button. It turned on as if nothing had been wrong before. He aimed the beam at where the figures had stood. Definitely gone. He pivoted and shone his light toward his house. He illuminated the back door, the windows, anywhere the intruders could be breaking in.

They weren't there.

"How the hell do they move so fast?" he whispered to

Boss. And so quietly? He hadn't even heard running foot-steps crunching the leaves. It was like they'd simply vanished rather than fled.

There was no telling how long these thugs would be satisfied just by scaring an old man and his dog. Eventually, they'd do something worse. Hurt him, or Geraldine. Wayne had to get to the bottom of this before that happened, with or without the police's help.

Wayne made a final sweep of the empty lot with his flashlight. He shivered and said, "Come on, Boss. Let's go back inside."

He returned to the house, already dreading tomorrow night's patrol.

Somethin' definitely ain't right.

1

There was always at least one, though this year there were three students dressed in Halloween costumes.

Rand Casey rarely got distracted when he was teaching, but he couldn't take his eyes off the outfits. He had a Taylor Swift, a guy in a gorilla suit complete with an oversized banana, and someone who he assumed was a character from a popular television show he didn't watch but had caught glimpses of when his daughter Libby had it on.

I really hate Halloween, Rand thought to himself as he clicked the button on his remote. The image on the screen at the front of the classroom changed to show two identical men wearing black suits and sunglasses.

"What do you think of when you see this picture?" Rand asked the class.

"Men in Black," someone said. Others snickered, likely assuming that wasn't the answer he was looking for.

"Correct," Rand said. "I think there is a considerable

lack of evidence around this topic and it's safe to say that Men in Black do *not* exist."

This was one of Rand's favorite lessons in his Intro to Supernatural Studies course and he always gave it near Halloween time. After all the supernatural and spiritual phenomena he taught in his class, he would eventually get the inevitable question: Is there anything you *don't* believe in?

Yes. Plenty. He'd put together an entire presentation on topics he considered nothing more than myths and urban legends. It usually turned into an interesting debate when he brushed up against someone's favorite conspiracy theory.

Rand felt strongly about this lesson. First, it was good to bring some lighthearted relief to the terrifying subject matter he usually taught. Second, if the purpose of his course was to equip his students with the knowledge they needed to defend themselves against dark supernatural forces, then it was equally important for them to know what *didn't* exist.

"You mean, like, the movie with Will Smith?" the student asked. "Of course that isn't real."

"The movie borrowed from the popular urban legend," Rand explained. "The Men in Black story has been around for a while. Just like in that film, it's said that they come in pairs, always dressed in black suits."

The student, the supposed Will Smith expert, seemed confused. "What do they want?"

"There are plenty of theories," Rand said. "People who claim to have been abducted by UFOs say Men in Black visited them and threatened them to keep quiet about what they experienced. Most believe the Men in Black work for a branch of government involved in secrecy and intelligence."

"Seems believable to me," the student said.

"Standard government secrecy and intelligence is believable," Rand said. "But sinister thugs that threaten UFO fanatics? No. The original abduction claims are shifty in the first place, so why would we believe that Men in Black approached them?"

A familiar hand in the front row shot into the air. "Is any of this going to be on the midterm?"

Rand chuckled. He'd tried to have a light lesson, but as always Stacy Thompson still worried about her 4.0. She eyed him though wide blue eyes, nervously fingering her shoulder-length blonde hair as she waited for his answer.

"No, Stacy. It wouldn't make sense to test you on myths and legends, don't you think?"

Stacy seemed to consider his words while lowering her hand.

Rand appreciated Stacy. Sometimes, she was the only person in the class to ask questions or participate in discussion.

The stadium classroom was more empty than full that day. Over half the students that had enrolled in his class at the beginning of the semester had dropped. That was common. Intro to Supernatural Studies wasn't difficult, but most students found it frightening.

"Next," Rand said, clicking his remote. The following image was of a tall humanoid wearing a suit. Its arms and legs were extra long, and it had a white, featureless face.

"Slenderman," muttered several students.

"Precisely. This guy's popular around the internet and arguably the most mainstream creepypasta out there."

"Creepypasta?" Stacy asked.

"Creepypasta is an internet slang term. It's from the word 'copy pasta,' which referred to text that went viral through emails and message boards back when the internet was young. Creepypasta refers to popular stories that circulate online that tell personal accounts of scary stories, strange incidents, and unexplained experiences, all of which are fictional, but written as if true." Rand gestured to the screen. "This guy took the 'net by storm in the early 2000s, and since then has launched an entire franchise— books, movies, and video games. It shows you the power of the internet these days. For as long has humans have been around, urban legends were handed down orally. Now, with a few clicks, a story can spread across the globe in less than an hour."

Rand clicked the remote again and Slenderman disappeared. He was replaced by two young children standing side-by-side, one taller than the other. They looked normal except for their eyes, which were completely black.

A student wearing sweatpants and an oversized t-shirt raised his hand. "Is it true you hate Halloween, Mr. Casey?"

"I'm glad you asked," Rand said, turning his back on the ominous-looking kids that loomed on the screen behind him. "Yes. Halloween is the most dangerous day of the year, and even though I know I can't control anyone, I would urge you all to stay inside."

Dozens of blank eyes stared at him. A few chuckles and murmurs flowed through the room.

"Oh… you're serious." The student smirked.

"Make fun of me all you like," Rand told them. He was

used to it. He had a sense of humor about most things, but Halloween was not one of them. "After all these months in this class, after all these lectures, what makes you think celebrating a day dedicated to witchcraft is a good idea? It's the one time of year where the world of the living and the dead are nearest, and only evil can come from that."

He was met by silence. The girl dressed as Taylor Swift was trying her best to stifle her laughter.

Rand ignored her and checked his watch. "Okay, that's it for today. You can all go."

"What about that?" Stacy asked, pointing toward the screen.

Rand looked over his shoulder. "Oh yeah. The black-eyed kids." He glanced at the time again. There were five minutes left in the class, but he wanted to get out of there early. "We can cover them tomorrow. Or maybe not. They say once you know about the black-eyed kids, you'll encounter them, so perhaps it's best if we ignore them altogether."

Stacy's face went white.

"Don't freak out, Stacy. This whole lesson is about things that *aren't* real, remember?"

Stacy didn't seem comforted. She couldn't look away from the picture. The black pools of their eyes seemed to draw her in.

Rand picked up on Stacy's fear and felt a pang of guilt. His class was for educational purposes, not a place to come for cheap, spooky thrills.

Rand used his remote to turn the screen off.

As the students gathered their belongings and filed out of the room, Rand packed his laptop and books into his bag, and slung it over his shoulder, and followed them out.

Rand had finished class early because he needed to check up on his daughter Libby and Tessa, Libby's mother, just to make sure they weren't planning anything for Halloween. Like his students, they also thought his distrust of Halloween was a bit over the top. He worried they might try to throw a costume party or plan something behind his back.

In Rand's opinion, the holiday was more dangerous than a category-five hurricane. And just like a hurricane, he had to make sure his family stayed indoors and safe.

2

The kitchen table was covered in notebooks and flash cards. A computer and a tablet rested near two Starbucks cups, one empty, the other half full. Stacy Thompson stared at all her study materials, feeling overwhelmed.

"This is too intense," Kim said. Stacy's roommate joined her at the kitchen table, sporting only a single notebook and a highlighter. She wore purple pajama pants and a white t-shirt. She used her hand to toss her wavy brown hair aside and out of her face. "How can you even find anything in all this stuff?"

"It's my ritual," Stacy shot back.

Kim looked confused as she scanned the paraphernalia. "Your ritual has gotten out of control. You need to rein it in. I don't know how you get stuff done."

Every semester, Stacy told herself she'd get more organized. Or maybe she needed to get more streamlined. She spent so much time prepping for study that she didn't actually get much studying done.

Less is more, she tried to tell herself. Though she stressed every semester before midterms, her process had yet to let her down. The dreaded B had never found its way into her grades.

"Are we studying or are you just going to make fun of me?" Stacy asked.

Kim opened her notebook and removed the cap from her highlighter, ready to go.

Stacy scanned through her supplies. On the edge of the table was the notebook she used for her Religion class, the only elective she had room for in her schedule that semester. The class was called Intro to Supernatural Studies, which was a misnomer because there wasn't a follow up course. She'd chosen it because it had a reputation for being easy. So far the tests had been simple, but studying was a challenge because the material frightened her.

"You can't be serious," Kim said.

Stacy looked up. "What?"

Kim had spotted Stacy's clearly labeled notebook. "You have a midterm in your ghost class? How is that even possible?"

"I think all classes are required to have a midterm."

"What could possibly be on a test in a class like that?" Kim went on, then smirked. "Or maybe you study for that class so much because of your huge teacher crush."

"Shut up," Stacy said. "I still need to study."

Kim rolled her eyes. "You have a photographic memory, and you've never made a B in your life."

While that sounded like an accomplishment, it only increased the pressure. Stacy had gotten straight As since she was five years old. The last thing she needed was to get her first B now.

"Are you going to the Boyd Street block party tomorrow night?" Kim asked, her notebook forgotten.

"Are you serious? There's no way I have time for that."

"Me neither, but I wouldn't miss it. It's a blast every year. I heard a group of students petitioned the university to move midterms away from Halloween weekend specifically because of the block party, but they got shot down."

"Midterms aren't something we can change, Kim. We need to study."

Kim sighed. "You sound just like one of *them*."

"One of who?"

The doorbell rang, taking Stacy by surprise.

"Did you invite Craig over?" she asked, then frowned and tossed aside her highlighter. "I thought we were supposed to focus on midterms tonight *without* extra company."

"Relax. I didn't invite him."

But Craig, Kim's current boyfriend, did have a habit of showing up unannounced. Stacy actually liked Craig, but that night he would be too much of a distraction.

Stacy pushed her chair out, the wooden legs screeching against the tile floor. She marched into the living room and threw open the front door.

"Craig, tonight isn't—"

No one was there.

Stacy stomped onto the porch and looked around. There was a chill in the air and a light breeze, so Stacy folded her arms and hunched her shoulders as she scanned the yard and street.

"Idiots," she whispered under her breath.

She and Kim rented a house in a small neighborhood near campus. The other houses nearby were also occupied by university students, which meant the area was far from peaceful. Every weekend so far that semester, one of their dumbass neighbors had thrown a party with enough booze to fuel it until the late morning hours. Stacy had wanted to move for a long time, but Kim liked the house. Stacy wanted to keep Kim as a roommate, so Stacy had to tolerate the noise. But that night, with midterms looming, she just couldn't handle any distractions.

But now, so close to Halloween, some extra disturbances were inevitable, starting with some immature moron ringing the doorbell and running away.

"You're only embarrassing yourself," Stacy called into the night, then went back inside, slamming the door behind her.

Another knock sounded at the door.

Stacy stopped dead. She slowly turned, furrowing her brow.

Impossible, she thought. The porch had been empty. How had someone come to the door that quickly?

She reached for the knob, but hesitated. A strange tingle blossomed at the base of her neck. She didn't know why, but this time she could sense a presence on the other side of the door.

Stacy took her hand away from the knob and leaned toward the peephole instead. Someone—no, *two* people, stood on her porch. Two *short* people, like children.

Maybe early trick-or-treaters? Stacy thought. There weren't any kids in their college neighborhood.

Stacy gripped the knob, turned it slowly. She cracked open the door.

She'd been right about them being children. The older boy looked about ten years old with unwashed, greasy brown hair. The red-and-white striped t-shirt and blue shorts he wore were smudged with grime, as if he'd been rolling around in a dumpster. The other boy, who looked to be about eight and was a head shorter, wore a black shirt and shorts with a thick mop of ginger hair, tangled and unkempt. Both were barefoot.

Where are their parents? Stacy wondered. *Where are their shoes?* Both kids had bare feet and their toes and ankles were caked with dried mud.

"Umm," Stacy began. "Hi." She peered over their heads and into the yard and street, searching for any sign of their parents.

"We need to come in and use your telephone," said the taller boy, staring straight at Stacy's chest. The other kid stared at her chest, too, although his hair hung over his eyes.

Perverts, Stacy thought, folding her arms over her chest.

"Where did you come from?" Stacy asked. "Where are your parents?"

"Your telephone," the older one said, as if growing angry.

"Umm… I don't have one. I only have a cell phone. It's in the kitchen, but if you wait here—"

"We need to come inside and use your telephone!" he shouted at her now, still staring at her chest. "We won't hurt you. We're not bad people."

Stacy recoiled at the sudden outburst. "I didn't say you were…"

Stacy's pulse thudded in her ears. Something wasn't right. Neither of the boys had moved since they'd arrived. They also didn't seem to mind the cold while wearing hardly any clothes, and their request sounded more like a threat.

"You're going to turn us away? We're two young kids who need help. Why would you do that?"

A roiling sensation in Stacy's gut left her wanting to vomit. She closed her eyes and swallowed, trying to fight off the sickness that had come over her so suddenly.

When she opened her eyes, both the boys met her gaze.

Stacy froze.

Their eyes were completely black. No iris, no pupil, no whites. Like two soulless black holes staring through her.

Stacy couldn't look away, drawn into their seemingly endless depth. She gripped the doorframe; in that moment, she just needed to touch something that she knew was grounded.

"You have to let us in," the older boy said. He spoke slowly, as if luring Stacy to obey. "We need help."

"No," she snapped. She grabbed the door and slammed it shut in their creepy faces. She threw the lock and deadbolt.

Now that the little freaks were out of sight, the feeling of nausea began to fade. She backed away from the door, expecting to hear another knock. Maybe some shouts from them. But so far, the boys hadn't reacted.

Stacy went to the living room window that had a view of the front porch. She nudged the curtain and peeked through. The little freaks were gone.

She exhaled a breath, letting the curtain fall back into place.

Stacy bolted to the kitchen, mind reeling from the bizarre occurrence on the porch.

"Kim."

Kim looked up from her notebook and cast Stacy a strange look. "Oh. You came back? I figured you gave up on studying and—" Kim straightened in her chair, eyes wide with alarm. "Stacy, are you all right? You look—"

Stacy jabbed her finger toward the door. "T-The kids from my class. The ones with black eyes."

"What are you talking about? What kids—"

"Kim, they're there. It's…"

Stacy felt tears coming. She had too much to say, but couldn't get it out fast enough.

Kim stood and went over to Stacy. She put her hands on Stacy's arms, and Stacy welcomed the touch—something that felt normal.

"You're shaking." Kim's face was close, concerned. "Slow down. Start at the beginning. Tell me where you went for so long."

"So long?" Stacy took a step backwards out of Kim's embrace. "Wh… what do you mean?"

Kim's eyebrows pulled together. "Stacy, you were gone for two hours."

3

R and crossed the quad and headed toward Campus Corner, the university's main coffee shop, with his bag slung over his shoulder. He breathed in the clear air of the chilly morning. It was shaping up to be a nice fall day, except for one major problem.

Halloween. It had finally arrived.

That alone kept Rand on edge. Anything could happen on Halloween. Whatever thin veil kept the world of the living and dead separate, it was thinnest on that night, and all manner of dark entities delighted in coming for him.

Shindael. The demon was never far behind. Rand hadn't seen him in a few days, but Rand was no idiot. Shindael would never give up tormenting him, and Halloween was the perfect opportunity.

Rand's plan was to approach the day as if it were normal and hope nothing went wrong. Coffee first, classes second, then make sure Libby and Tessa were safe inside for the night, and finally return home and stay there until the next morning.

Simple. Except it rarely ever was on Halloween.

Campus Corner was a small place with a relaxed vie, if a bit pretentious. The manager regularly rotated mediocre paintings by the university's art students, and as usual some guy plucked away at his guitar in the corner, soft notes filling the cafe. Rand hoped he wouldn't start singing.

When Rand walked in, he was met with a decorative plastic skeleton and ghost dangling from the ceiling, swaying in the breeze that snuck in from outside. Rand glided around them, keeping his distance as if they were diseased.

"Good morning, Mr. Rand," said the barista Cassie, who was always there for the morning shift. She must've only taken afternoon classes. She'd added a pink streak to her short blonde hair since Rand had seen her last. "Happy Halloween."

"What have you done to the place?" Rand gestured toward the hanging decorations—pumpkins, spiders, monsters, zombies. "It's usually so nice in here."

"Ted made me put all that up before we opened this morning," Cassie said, rolling her eyes. "But whatever. It's Halloween. I guess we can have some fun."

Rand grimaced. Cassie rang up his black Americano from memory.

"I'll bring it out to you," Cassie said as Rand handed her cash.

"Thanks, Cassie."

Rand went to the patio to enjoy the nice weather—and to get away from the guitar player who'd started humming into the microphone. The outdoor section was adorned with plants and had a stone water feature that Rand found particularly relaxing.

Rand sat down at the only remaining empty table and leaned back in his chair. His phone chimed in his pocket. When he slid it out, he had a text from his friend Miller.

Happy Halloween Rando.

The text was followed by all the possible relevant emojis: ghost, devils, zombies, aliens, pumpkins.

Rand rolled his eyes. Even Miller made fun of him for his hatred of Halloween, though the man knew first-hand how dangerous it could be.

He'd better stay inside tonight, too, Rand thought. He made a mental note to swing by Miller's shop and make sure he wasn't making plans for the night.

Cassie brought his coffee, and the warm cup in his hand felt pleasant against the chilly morning. Rand sipped it, savoring the steaming bitterness.

"Is it okay?" Cassie asked.

"It always is when you make it, Cassie," Rand said.

The girl beamed and lingered near his table. "So what are you going to be for Halloween this year, Mr. Rand?"

"I'm going to be asleep with the doors locked and the lights off."

"Oh, that's no fun. Why don't you come to the Boyd Street block party? That's where I'll be." She glanced toward the unattended counter inside the coffee shop. A line was forming in her absence.

"I think I'm a little old for something like that."

"I saw Mr. Galway there last year. He was dressed like a mummy."

Rand didn't know Jim Galway from the Math depart-

24

ment personally, but was aware of his reputation for perving on the young female students. Boyd Street would be right up that guy's alley.

"Please be careful tonight, Cassie," Rand said. He wanted to lecture her about how she would be better off staying indoors, but didn't feel like opening that can of worms while his coffee was still hot.

"Of course. But not *too* careful. I don't want to miss all the fun." She gave Rand a wry smile before she went back inside.

Rand shook his head. Cassie was another lost cause, a Halloween lover. He couldn't save them all.

Rand picked up his phone to respond to Miller. But before he could, someone else appeared by his side.

It was Stacy Thompson. Her face was pinched and her eyes glistened with tears.

"Oh. Hey, Stacy. Are you—"

"Mr. Casey, I need to talk to you." She seemed a bit more on edge than usual.

"Is it about the midterm? Stacy, I don't think you need to worry—"

"No, it isn't about the midterm," she shrieked. She caught herself and looked over her shoulder to see if she'd drawn any attention. A few nearby heads had turned. When she looked back to Rand, she forced a whisper. "Please. I need to talk to you right now."

"Okay," Rand said, softening his tone and straightening in his chair. "Have a seat."

Stacy again scanned the other students filling the nearby tables. "Can we go somewhere more private?"

"Oh. Um… sure." Rand grabbed his coffee cup and followed Stacy through the coffee shop's patio entrance and out onto the street where no one else was around.

"What's going on?" Rand asked her.

Stacy wiped away a tear. "I saw them last night."

"Saw who?"

"Those kids you had on the screen in class yesterday. The ones with black eyes. They showed up at my door."

"But Stacy," Rand said. "Those things aren't real."

Stacy Thompson deflated. "Come on. After everything you've taught us, *you're* going to be the one to not believe me?"

"Whoa," Rand said. "It's not that I don't believe you, it's just..." She seemed on the verge of breaking down, and he realized perhaps he'd been too thoughtless with what he'd said. His daughter *had* told him dozens of times that he sometimes didn't think before he spoke. "Why don't you tell me the whole story."

Stacy shuddered. "I don't even want to think about it."

"The only way I can help you is if I hear your story. Don't leave anything out."

The way Stacy had come to Rand just now was the same way his past clients did after they'd had a terrifying encounter they couldn't explain. Rand needed to start off the same way he always did: by hearing the story. Often, supernatural explanations could be debunked just from the stories alone.

The lanky, curly-haired guitar player from the coffee shop passed through the patio's gate and in between Rand and Stacy. He carried his guitar case and focused on his cell phone, texting as he walked by, oblivious to the tense silence he'd just disrupted.

Stacy waited until he was out of earshot. "I was at

home. My roommate Kim was with me. We were supposed to study, but the doorbell rang."

They most often arrive at the door, Rand thought, remembering the few stories of the black-eyed kids he'd studied.

"I thought it was Kim's boyfriend, so I got up to answer the door, and they were standing there. No, wait." She paused. "No one was there the first time. I thought it was someone playing a prank, so I went back inside and closed the door, but then someone knocked. And it was weird, Mr. Casey, because no one was there and then the knock just happened. Like, there wasn't even time for someone to come up to the door."

Rand frowned. What Stacy had just described was quite common with supernatural phenomenon. He'd experienced it himself many times. Entities didn't need to walk up to your door. They just appeared.

"When I opened the door again, they were there." A tear escaped from her eye and she wiped it away.

"When did you notice that their eyes were black?" he asked. Stacy seemed thrown off by the sudden question. To Rand, her response mattered.

"Um… Not right away. I don't know how I missed it. They weren't looking me in the eye at first. Just kind of staring straight ahead. And I just started to feel weird. Sick. Like I wanted to throw up. Or like they were hypno-tizing me. Something like that."

Rand pursed his lips. These were all details that he'd studied in previous sightings. The victim always reported a trance-like state that began once the kids had appeared. This caused them to not immediately notice the black eyes. After the encounter was over, the victim surmised that the black-eyed kids were trying to keep the victim from noticing their eyes. As if the kids knew that their unnatural eyes were what would keep the victim from allowing them inside.

"Did they speak to you?" Rand asked. *And did they say they needed a telephone*, he thought.

"Yes. They wanted to come in and use my telephone."

Stacy watched him, waiting for his next question. Rand knew what he needed to ask next, and he dreaded the answer.

"Did you let them in?"

"No."

Rand let out the breath he'd been holding.

"Why? What happens when you let them in?"

He didn't know. No one seemed to know. In the few accounts of the black-eyed kids that existed, all the victims had been able to break out of the so-called trance and refuse to let the kids in. That was one reason why Rand had always considered the black-eyed kids to be a myth. There were no *real* endings to the stories. No one had ever let them in, so he didn't know what happened when they came inside, or what the black-eyed kids wanted in the first place.

"They freaked me out so bad that I slammed the door on them. Then they disappeared. But then…"

"Then what?" Rand asked.

"But when I went back to the kitchen, my roommate Kim said I'd been gone for two whole hours. And according to the clock, she was right. But my conversation with the kids felt like it had only lasted for a few minutes. It was so weird."

Distorted time, Rand thought. That was never a good

28

sign. He'd experienced it himself on a number of occasions.

"Say something," Stacy pleaded.

"What you've told me sounds a lot like the accounts I've studied," Rand replied, speaking slowly and carefully. He didn't want to frighten Stacy more than she already was.

"I thought you said they weren't real."

"I've never encountered them in my practice," Rand said. "And the stories I've come across need a… lot more corroboration, in my opinion."

"Well, I have all the corroboration you need now."

This was an interesting situation. Rand had never before worked with a client that he'd known personally. For that reason, all were subject to a little bit of skepticism before he began a full-blown investigation into their claims. But Stacy Thompson was different. He'd never known the girl to make up stories, lie, or seek attention.

"Did you do any more reading about the black-eyed kids after class?" Rand asked.

"No," she said. Her eyes honed in on him. "You don't believe me."

"I do believe that you saw something that made you feel that way," Rand said, choosing his words carefully. "But you have to keep in mind that there's a process I follow when someone approaches me with stories like this."

Stacy rubbed her fingers into her eyes. "Fine. Can you at least tell me what I should do?"

"What were you planning to do tonight?" Rand asked.

"Hide in my room."

"If you hadn't seen anything last night, what would you have done?"

"Study, of course."

"Okay. That sounds good. But I wouldn't recommend you to be alone. You need to be around people." Any entity seeking to frighten or attack their target almost always waited until the individual was alone.

Stacy's gaze lingered on the fall display that had been set up near the entrance to the coffee shop's patio. Stacked blocks of hay were topped with jack-o-lanterns. "My roommate has been begging me to go with her to the Boyd Street block party."

Rand grimaced. "That won't work. You need to stay inside where it's safe."

"But if I stay home, then I'll be alone. You just said I needed to be around people. There'll be *hundreds* of people on Boyd Street tonight."

"Right, but…"

"But what?"

"You shouldn't leave the house on Halloween."

"That's just you being paranoid about the holiday. You told us yesterday in class that you hate it. The problem is these kids, not the day of the year."

"Can you talk your roommate or another one of your friends into staying home with you tonight?" Rand asked.

Stacy scoffed. "Yeah right. It's the biggest party of the year."

"Well…"

Maybe the Boyd Street block party would be the lesser of two evils for Stacy, Rand though. *Just this once.*

"Will you help me?" Stacy's face softened, as if she was nervous that he might tell her no.

"Of course," Rand said. "There's a reason for what you saw, and we'll get to the bottom of it."

"How? What will you do? Is this going to be like…"

Be like the cases I talk about in class? Rand thought. *I hope not. But I can't yet say for sure.*

"Don't tell me you don't know what to do," she said.

"I do," Rand said. Actually, it would be more accurate to say that he knew where to start.

Miller.

Rand's friend Miller Landingham had dug up info on every urban legend known to man. Surely he had some information or insight pertaining to the black-eyed kids.

"I'll discuss this with a colleague. We'll make a plan of action and go from there."

Stacy deflated. That didn't seem to be practical enough for her. "But what if they come back before you can do anything?"

"That's why I'm urging you to be around people," Rand said. "Just for tonight. Tomorrow, I'll have something more concrete for you."

Rand understood Stacy's dissatisfaction. He truly did. But he had to approach this carefully. If Stacy had indeed had an encounter with the black-eyed kids, then the situation was unprecedented to Rand.

His own fear had begun to creep in, as if he were absorbing it from Stacy. He would have taken it all from her if he could have. Despite all that he'd experienced, Rand had never claimed to be immune to fear, and he never would. But when a brand-new situation caused him to feel fear, he knew that was just another liability—entities could, and would use it against him. They had before.

Stacy looked at her watch. Her knees buckled. "I'm late

for Calculus. Ugh. Today was supposed to be a midterm review class."

"Go," Rand told her. "I'll be in touch after I speak with my colleague. Call me if anything happens. Anything at all."

"I need your number."

Stacy handed Rand her phone and he typed in his number. He handed it back to her and she called his phone. When her number popped up on Rand's screen, he declined the call and saved her as a contact.

"Don't leave your phone on silent tonight," Stacy said.

"Try to relax, Stacy. Everything is going to be okay."

She flashed a hint of an eye roll, as if she'd like to believe what he said, but didn't. "You sound just like Kim. I can't even relax when creepy kids *don't* show up at my door." She sighed. "Anyway. Just help me. I still feel really weird about what happened."

"I'm here for you, Stacy."

She tried to smile, but it only came out as small twitch of her lips.

Rand watched her go, frowning. He always hated it when someone had their first negative interaction with the spiritual world. The trauma could last a lifetime. Stacy Thompson didn't deserve what had happened to her, and he would do anything he could to help her.

Fucking Halloween, he thought.

4

The final bell rang and the halls of Denton High School filled with teenagers clamoring for the freedom of the Halloween weekend. Libby Casey was among them. She rummaged through her locker, skimming the spines of her textbooks. Her teachers had been generous and hadn't assigned much homework for Halloween night, but Libby started shoving half her books into her backpack anyway.

Her locker slammed closed, almost catching her arm like a biting steel trap. Her friend Bailey's hand was pressed on the locker door, fingers spread.

"He asked me." Bailey said, beaming.

"Terrence?"

"Yes. Finally. It took him long enough. I was *this* close to flexing my inner modern woman and asking him to the Halloween dance myself."

A black-and-orange banner hung above Libby's locker.

"DENTON HIGH HALLOWEEN DANCE. ALL GOBLINS AND GHOULS INVITED."

Bailey had had her eye on Terrance as a date for two weeks. She'd dropped all kinds of hints, and Libby had had to hear about every single one. As the dance drew closer, she'd started to get paranoid that he wouldn't ask her. She'd even started dressing up more for school—today she wore a hint of mascara and she'd curled her brown hair, eschewing her normal single braid.

"That's what I told you to do in the first place," Libby said. "You knew he was shy. You could've just shown him how it's done and not wasted a bunch of time."

"Doesn't matter now," Bailey said. "Oh, and he's cool with going in our group." She eyed Libby's full backpack. "Planning on getting much homework done at the dance?"

"I need the books for the plan," Libby said. She opened her locker again and crammed more textbooks into her backpack. Bailey watched with an amused grin as Libby struggled to pull the zipper over the protruding edges of the hardcovers.

"Right. The *plan*. It's all about the *plan*. You've been telling me all week that you needed a plan. Do you finally have one?"

"I do. So listen up, because if it doesn't go just right, then I won't be able to go to the dance."

They started down the hall toward the exit, shouldering past thick groups of students like they were trying to push to the front of a concert crowd. Libby had to raise her voice over the din of conversations so her friend could hear her.

"First, we'll go to Bill's house." Bill was Libby's soon-to-be stepdad, and her mom had moved into his house.

"I'll lay all these books and notebooks out on the table like the most intense study session you've ever seen. When my dad shows up, the story is that we're staying in all night to study."

Bailey listened, waiting for more. When she realized that was the end, she shot Libby a confused look. "That's it? Libby, that's called a lie, not a plan."

"That's just the first part," Libby said. "If my dad buys it, then we're done. But I've also planned for other... contingencies."

Bailey lifted her eyebrows. "Like?"

"Well, if he lurks around my Bill's house like a prison guard and makes sure no one leaves, then we'll have to sneak out the back door, in costume, and cross the neighbor's yard to get out of the neighborhood. Then, we'll walk to your house, where you'll have parked your car, and we can use it to get to the dance.

"There's also a chance he'll show up to the dance and look for me if he finds out about it, though right now he doesn't know. I've already paid Victoria Lansing fifty bucks to be on the lookout." Victoria was the student body president and had organized the Halloween dance. She'd told Libby that she planned to spend the entire dance at the door checking to make sure costumes weren't inappropriate or that no one was trying to come into the dance drunk. "I gave her a picture of my dad, so she'll know what he looks like. She'll send me a warning text if she see's him, then I'll run out the gym's back door by the locker rooms.

"Oh, then there's my mom. She and Bill have their own party tonight at Bill's office, so if my dad catches them instead, there's a chance he can convince my mom to tell him—"

"Jeez, Libby," Bailey said. "Seriously? I always thought Mr. Rand was a cool dad."

"Three hundred and sixty-four days a year, he's the best I could ever hope for," Libby said. "But when it comes to Halloween, he has a strict no-tolerance policy. No celebrating, no leaving the house. I'm the only person I know who's never been trick-or-treating."

Bailey may never understand, but Libby *absolutely* needed a plan if she was going to make it to that Halloween dance. All throughout the week, every time Libby's attention in class had drifted off and she'd considered each potential way her dad could catch her out of the house on Halloween night, a heavy load of guilt burdened her. She, more than anyone else, understood why her dad was so averse to Halloween. What most people considered a fun holiday was a perfect time for evil spirits to stir.

When Libby had firmly decided to seize Halloween for herself that year, to finally experience it like a normal person for once, she knew she'd need a well-thought-out plan to get away with it.

The stakes were high. If she was caught, then not only would her dad be very angry, he would also be very hurt. He had the highest expectations for Libby, and she knew he would feel very betrayed.

Mrs. Worsham, the oldest teacher on staff and a decade past normal retirement age, stood at the front door of the school in the middle of the exit, forcing the students to divert around her as if she were a rock in a river.

"Don't drink and drive. Don't do drugs," she shouted through hands cupped around her mouth. Everyone, including Libby and Bailey, tuned her out as they left the building.

The afternoon was clear, and Libby welcomed the chilled air as she emerged from the stuffy, crowded hallway. Outside, some students dispersed to their cars while others piled into the school busses lined up at the edge of the parking lot. Libby could smell their familiar exhaust.

"I still think you're giving too much thought to this plan," Bailey said. They could hear each other better now that they didn't have to talk over the crowd of students and Mrs. Worsham's dire warnings. "Oh, I forgot to tell you that Terrence and I are going to dress up as skeletons for the dance. After he asked me he told me he didn't have a costume, so I said he could borrow the skeleton outfit my brother wore last year. I'll wear mine again and we can match."

"Oh, about the costumes," Libby began. "We'll need to pack a bag of normal clothes to change into in case my dad—"

Strong arms wrapped around Libby from behind, and she shrieked. An icy chill shot through her body as she scrambled out of the unwelcome grasp. She whirled around and saw Parker Haney behind her, confused yet amused.

"Whoa. You okay?" he said. His smile widened, showing his perfectly straight teeth.

"Parker. Sorry. You scared the crap out of me." Libby's skin prickled as the sudden, sharp dose of adrenaline began to fade. She rubbed at her arms to make the icky feeling go away.

"My bad." Although he didn't seem too sorry.

Libby herself was surprised by the fierce, instinctive reaction. It was more than just being startled. The last time she'd been grabbed from behind, she'd been locked up in an attic by a psychotic man during her dad's previous case.

"We all good for tonight?" Parker asked.

"Yeah." She took a calming breath to settle her nerves.

Parker Haney was captain of the swim team, had wavy, sandy-colored hair and an athletic body and he made good grades. According to Bailey, Parker was utterly perfect. Libby wasn't that single-minded about him, but she did like him. When word began percolating through the school that she and Justin Tidwell had broken up, Parker wasted no time inviting her to the Halloween dance.

"You said you'd be at your stepdad's house, right?" Parker said. "You still need to text me his address."

"Yes." But then Libby remembered the intricate parts of her plan that she hadn't shared with Parker. "Or we might be at Bailey's."

"But I thought…" He shrugged. "Whatever. Just let me know. See you later on."

Parker left them and joined a group of his buddies on the other side of the parking lot.

"What's with the freak out?" Bailey asked, giving her a look. "It's physically impossible to be repulsed by Parker Haney."

"It reminded me of that time… He just scared me. Forget it."

"And I see you haven't clued him in on your little plan," Bailey said as they walked toward Libby's car.

"We barely know each other. I don't want him thinking I have a crazy dad. It's only today that he's like this. The rest of the time he's fine. But I'd like to make a good impression on Parker, so if you don't mind keeping my dad's paranoia a little secret between us, that'd be great."

"You got it," Bailey said.

"So we'll go to Bill's house now," Libby said. Bill was Libby's soon-to-be stepfather. Her mom had moved in with her fiancé. "I'll call my dad from the landline so he knows I'm there, give him the cover story, and have Mom talk to him so she can corroborate. She'll get a lecture about how I'm not to leave the house, blah, blah, blah." Bailey started scrolling her phone as Libby continued explaining. "Meanwhile, we'll set up the living room to look like we're studying, because no matter what my mom says, my dad *will* still show up. Then, we'll—"

Libby's phone vibrated in her back pocket. When she checked the text message, she saw it was from her friend Georgia Collins.

"Hey Libby! I need u to meet me at the hospital. I need to talk to u…"

Libby's heart thudded. Georgia had cystic fibrosis and spent most of her time at St. Mary's hospital. Libby had first met Georgia when Libby's dad removed a demon that had attached itself to the sick girl.

"Is everything okay?" Libby sent the response, and immediately the three dots started bouncing on the screen.

"Can u come by the hospital? Like now? Ur out of school right? I've been waiting all day."

Libby chewed her lip. That didn't really work with her plans.

"Can I call you?"

"I want to tell u in person."

"What's wrong?" Libby heard Bailey ask. "Who texted you?"

Libby's tight plan hadn't allowed any room for diversions. Visiting Georgia now would put her behind schedule.

But what if Georgia had gotten some bad news about her health? Or was she experiencing supernatural activity again? Was it both?

"It won't take long." Georgia texted again. But Libby knew how talkative Georgia could be.

Libby decided she had to go see Georgia at St. Mary's. It was the right thing to do.

"Be there in 15."

Georgia sent back a thumbs-up emoji.

"Um, Bailey," Libby said. "Little change of plans. I have a quick errand to run."

"You said you'd drive me home." Bailey's face fell.

"I know, but this is an emergency. I think."

Georgia was usually fine with texts, calls, Instagram messages, video chats—all of it. But now she wanted to speak to Libby in person. Given the terrifying circumstances that had brought them together, Libby just couldn't put her friend off when she seemed so desperate.

"What about your big scheme to trick your dad?" Bailey asked.

"I'll just have to risk it." Libby popped her trunk and her backpack, heavy with textbooks, made a loud *thunk* when she dropped it in.

"Just don't leave me hanging," Bailey said as Libby climbed into her car. "As Parker Haney's date to the Halloween dance, you have a responsibility to all females at Denton High to—"

Libby couldn't help but grin as she closed the car door, cutting off her friend's speech.

5

St. Mary's Medical Center was the largest hospital in the city. It was pristine, highly regarded, and seemed protected by an aura of Catholic iconography and signs that promised faith-based healing combined with the practices of modern medicine. As Libby walked down those familiar pristine hallways, only terrible memories came back to her. She passed the chapel and chills coursed through her body. It wasn't so long ago that a horrible demon had chased her and Georgia through those same corridors.

Georgia had told Libby to meet her in the "Healing Garden," which was a huge outdoor area behind the hospital, filled with trees, fountains, and flowers in the spring. Libby followed the cobbled sidewalk, searching for her friend. Other patients were out and about, going for a stroll with a nurse in attendance.

Libby spotted her friend off the main walkway. Georgia sat on a bench underneath a sprawling oak tree, reading a book. Her eyes were shaded by large sunglasses that made her look like a fly. Her oxygen tank leaned against the bench beside her, cannula running from its spout to her nostrils.

Georgia looked up as Libby approached, smiled, then stood.

"I haven't seen you in forever," Georgia said when they hugged.

Apparently, to Georgia, "forever" meant a few weeks.

"Sorry. School's been crazy," Libby said.

"You mentioned you got caught up in your dad's last case," Georgia said. "But you never told me the story. I posted, like, eleven things on Instagram and you didn't comment on any of them. That was my first clue that you were in trouble. Sorry I didn't come and rescue you myself. Are you all right?"

"More or less. But what about you? You were really freaking me out with those messages. What's going on?"

The light went out of Georgia's eyes just a little. Georgia sat on the bench and Libby joined her. Georgia *seemed* normal, at least. Or, rather, as normal as could be expected. She didn't look weaker, or sicker, or like she was struggling.

Georgia peered ahead toward the garden's small pond and Libby followed her gaze. Next to it, an elderly man wearing a hospital gown lifted his hand and waved. Georgia returned the gesture. "That's Mr. Vincent."

She's stalling, Libby realized. "Close friend of yours?"

"We chat when we bump into each other. He likes to feed the fish in that pond."

Georgia adjusted her nasal cannula. "I actually wanted to talk to your dad about this, but I thought I'd run it by you first."

"Have there been any other *incidents*?" Libby asked, the words coming slowly.

"Nothing like that," Georgia said, fingering the plastic tube. "Thank God. But there have been other interesting changes…"

"Like…"

Georgia watched an elderly woman being pushed along the walkway in her wheelchair by a caretaker. She waited for the woman to pass out of earshot. "I see things."

"What do you see?"

"People."

Libby now realized where this was probably going. "And… what kind of people?"

"Are you *really* going to make me quote *The Sixth Sense*? I think you know what I mean."

"Yeah, I do, but is it like last time?"

"No no no. Not at all."

Georgia Collins had been through a lot. Libby had first met the girl through a series of unfortunate circumstances that led Georgia's parents to contact Libby's dad. There was a demonic infestation in St. Mary's, and Georgia was the one who'd discovered the entity. The situation had quickly spiraled out of control.

"Last time, it was that asshole demon talking directly to me," Georgia explained. "Now, I only see… well, I'm not sure how to describe it. They're just happening, like a movie. I'll see an old man walking down the hall, and he doesn't look like he belongs. Sometimes I see people dressed up in old-fashioned nurse uniforms. They're going about their business, ignoring me and everyone else."

"Ghosts," Libby said.

"Yeah. Your dad mentioned once that there are probably tons of ghosts here, because lots of people die in hospitals."

"He's right. This place is overflowing with highly charged emotional energy here."

That was how Libby's dad had explained it to her. The ghosts, the spirits of the people that Georgia was seeing, had a strong connection to St. Mary's during their life. By the sounds of it, she was seeing both patients and employees that had passed.

"I remember when you brought that medium to my room for a séance," Georgia went on. She rhythmically traced the edge of the bench with the tip of her index finger. "She could see the spirits all around us, and she communicated with them, too."

Georgia was talking about Katie, who used to work with Libby's dad on cases. Katie was sensitive to the spiritual world and could contact spirits more readily than her dad could. Katie and Libby's dad had also dated for a short time, though it had been one of his messier break ups.

"Some people, like that medium, are very sensitive to things that most people cannot see," Libby said.

Georgia stopped tracing the edge of the bench and wiped her hand on her jeans. "What if I'm one of them?"

"It's possible," Libby said. "Because…"

"Because why?"

Libby hesitated.

"Because I'm so close to the end?"

Georgia didn't have a problem calling it like it was. Because of her cystic fibrosis, Georgia was never meant to have a long life. If she were lucky and didn't have any serious complications, she could expect to live until her thirties.

"That's not always the case," Libby said, "but yes, people who are closer to death often see those who have already passed on but are still lingering."

"I did some internet research and read the same thing online."

"Be careful with what you read online about that kind of stuff. There are some crazies out there who don't really understand what they're talking about. Or what they're messing around with."

"My doctors say the same thing when I tell them I read about my symptoms online."

"If they're just ghosts, then they won't hurt you. Like the lady in the nurse's uniform you're talking about. She probably worked here when she was alive. When she died, her spirit wasn't ready to let go. Now she walks the halls, repeating her day-to-day activities because she doesn't even realize she's dead."

Libby knew that demons, on the other hand, were far worse. They were inhuman spirits that intentionally caused chaos, fear, and sometimes even death.

"That's really sad," Georgia said, voice dropping.

"Yeah."

"Do you think since I can see her, I could also talk to her? Maybe help her move on to the next life? Isn't that what mediums do?"

I have to be careful how I respond, Libby thought. Her dad always advised people to never mess around with the other world, and he was right. The realms of the living and the dead were never meant to intersect.

46

"I don't think that's a good idea," Libby said. "Once you do that, you'll give off a certain aura. Other spirits will pick up on it and know that you are able and willing to communicate with them. They won't leave you alone. They might reach out, and you definitely don't want that. Because once you start, you can't stop it."

Libby's dad had dealt with dozens of cases that started just like that—people who were clairvoyant enough to see spirits making efforts to communicate with them.

Georgia stared at the grass between her feet, considering. The sun had begun to set, and Libby rubbed the goosebumps that had sprouted on her arms.

"What if I *do* want to communicate with these spirits?" Georgia asked.

Libby hesitated while she chose her words carefully. "That's a huge decision, Georgia. Once you open those doors, they're hard to close."

Georgia sniffled, and the first tears appeared at the corners of her eyes.

"Oh." Libby put a hand on her friend's shoulder. "Are you okay?"

"Yeah, yeah," Georgia said, wiping her eyes. "It's just… I'm going to die. Well, everyone dies, but I'm going to die before everyone else. I'm sick and that's not going to change. I won't grow up and be a politician who makes all these laws that fix the country. I won't get to be a famous artist or musician. Or a police officer, or a teacher, or the greatest female boxer to ever live. I'm *never* going to grow up."

Libby's own eyes began to fill with tears. Her friend had come to terms with her short life, and Libby had always assumed that Georgia had also handled all the emotions that came with it. Libby now realized that she'd been mistaken.

"Maybe this is a way I can help people. Kind of like your dad, except with less scary stuff. That medium he brought over… she helps people. Since I have this ability, I can start helping people. Because if I'm going to give anything back to the world, it has to be now. Otherwise, what did my life mean? I was born sick, lived sick, sucked up a bunch of valuable food and water and air, all to just die. I can't do that." She wiped her eyes and cheeks with her shirt. "I accepted a long time ago that I'm going to die, but what I haven't accepted is me dying without doing something great."

Libby took a deep breath before answering. "I hear you. Everything you said makes sense. But before you make any decisions, talk to my dad. He can guide you better than me."

"Yeah. But I wanted to tell you first. Just to get your take on it."

"You were right to do that," Libby said. "My dad is crazy right now with Halloween coming up. He always loses his mind this time of year."

"He's not a fan, is he?"

"The understatement of the century."

"I'll call him November first, then."

"Make it November second."

"If you say so. Oh, it looks like Mr. Victor made a new friend." The man was chatting to another patient that had walked near the pond. "Other people can see Victor. That means he's not a ghost. See? I'm already an expert medium."

Libby smirked. "Just promise me you won't try to

48

reach out to any of those spirits until you speak to my dad," Libby said.

"Fine. I promise." Georgia held out her pinky and Libby wrapped it with her own. "So, wait, you have a new boyfriend now. Already?"

"He isn't a boyfriend."

"What happened to the last guy?" Georgia asked. Libby winced. "Oh, wait… he's the reason you got kidnapped, right? Yeah, definitely a good thing y'all aren't together anymore. You never sent me a picture of this one."

"I'll show you one quickly before I go." Libby pulled her phone out of her pocket and opened her camera roll. "Denton's Halloween dance is tonight and I have a whole thing planned out so my dad doesn't catch me."

Libby showed Georgia the picture Parker used for his Instagram profile. He faced off center with a blurry background. The lighting was just right.

Georgia studied it. "No. Don't like him."

Libby's mouth fell open. "You're literally the first person who's said that about him."

"Don't care. He's not right for you."

Libby chuckled at her friend's staunch declaration. "And how do you know?"

"I can just tell."

Libby stood and put her phone back into her pocket. "As much as I'd love to stick around and hear why"—and admittedly she *was* curious about Georgia's reasoning—"I have to be on my way. If my dad finds out what I'm up to, he'll kill me."

"Good luck with that," Georgia said. "And if he does kill you, it won't be the worst thing in the world. At least I'll still be able to talk to you."

6

R and drove straight from campus to Miller Landingham's bookstore. He'd wanted to cancel his classes and get there sooner, because he considered what Stacy had told him an emergency. However, with his recent and extended absence due to his previous case, he was already on thin ice with the department head.

Rand burst through the bookshop door, nearly knocking the jingling bell out from where it was bolted into the ceiling. For possibly the first time, he was not the only person there. A single shopper—a middle-aged woman—was browsing the shelves of used books. Miller stood nearby, hovering awkwardly, waiting for some sort of query. Rand knew Miller was not accustomed to having shoppers and didn't quite know how to act.

The frantic jingling got Miller's attention. His annoyed gaze darted between Rand and the bell, no doubt wondering why his friend had nearly ripped the thing from the plaster.

Rand jabbed his finger toward Miller's office. Miller nodded toward his precious customer. Rand, however, ignored him and charged behind the checkout counter and through the door that led to the back of the bookshop.

The office contained Miller's whole life. All the documents for his business overflowed from drawers in his computer desk. Boxes of books he hadn't yet shelved were stacked along the wall. His single mattress and comforter were in the corner, the closest thing he had to a bedroom at the moment. A phone charger dangled from the nearby plug. The smell of fried food, likely from lunchtime, lingered.

Miller shuffled inside the office behind Rand. His black, disheveled hair was greasier than usual and his cheeks and neck were covered in coarse stubble. "I have a customer. Can't this wait until after she's gone?"

"One of my students had an encounter."

Miller paused and appeared to digest what Rand had said. He closed the office door. "An encounter with what?"

"Do you know anything about the black-eyed kids?"

Miller waved his hand. "Those are just an urban legend, Rando."

"That's what I thought," Rand said. "They're in my 'stuff I don't believe in' lecture I gave yesterday. This morning, though, one of my students approached me in the campus coffee shop, scared out of her mind, saying black-eyed kids showed up on her doorstep the night before."

"You're kidding." Miller took off his glasses and rubbed each lens with a section of his red-and-white plaid shirt pinched between two fingers. "You sure she was telling the truth? Not just trying to mess with you? I know not all your students believe in the stuff you teach."

"Stacy Thompson would be the last person to do something like that," Rand said.

Miller replaced his glasses and sat in his chair near the computer. "She didn't let them in, did she?"

"No, thank God. That's their thing, right? They always want to come inside the house."

"It's not in all the stories, but it features prominently in most."

"What stories have you read?"

"I've found accounts online of people who've encountered these things. Most are very similar. There's a knock at the door, doesn't matter what time of day, and it's two kids. They usually stand out in a jarring way. Like their clothes don't match the current fashion trends, or they look dirty. Sometimes they even smell. But they always say they need to come inside your house."

"That's about all I cover in my lecture," Rand said. "Although I know there has to be more to it."

On a nearby table was a box that did not match the others in the office. It was plain brown, while all the rest were stamped with the blue logo of Miller's book store's distributor. The cardboard flaps were not sealed. Curious, Rand flipped one open.

"Don't look in there!" Miller shouted.

Rand jerked his hand back as if burned and gave Miller a questioning look. "What is it?"

"It's an early Christmas gift." Miller rubbed the back of his head. "For you."

"Since when can you afford gifts?"

"I can't. So you better smile and love it when you get it."

Rand distanced himself from the off-limits box in two long, deliberate strides. "Anyway. Have you collected any information about these kids?"

"I've gathered some things, but I tend to skip over most." Miller swiveled in his chair and jiggled the computer mouse to wake up the screen. "Since the stories are almost identical, it feels like they're from internet trolls." He double clicked through a maze of folders on his hard drive.

"Why do they ask to come in? Why don't they just walk in?"

"It seems they have to be invited," Miller said.

"Like vampires?"

"Yeah, but we both know vampires aren't real."

Rand raised his eyebrows. "Well, yesterday I said the same thing about black-eyed kids. What happens if you let them in?"

Miller straightened in his chair and slowly turned to face him. "Now that I think about it, I've never seen an account where that's happened."

"Stacy asked me the same thing, and I didn't have an answer."

"Here's something," Miller said, opening a document. It took several seconds to load on the aged, lagging machine. Once it appeared, Miller skimmed the text, lips moving as he read. "What I have here is the first credited online post about them that appeared in 1996."

"That's why I'd always considered them an urban legend," Rand said. "Real demons have been known for millennia, but the black-eyed kids weren't ever written about until the internet came around."

"I agree," Miller said. "This story is interesting because it doesn't have them coming to the door. They approached the guy while he was waiting in his parked car. The kids knocked on the window and asked him for a ride. He tried to ask them questions, but they wouldn't answer. They only demanded that he let them into the car. Then he noticed that their eyes were completely black. He was so scared he drove off right away."

"Same basic concept," Rand said. "They wanted inside."

"Exactly. What else…" Miller skimmed the document. "They often come in pairs. That's another common fixture of the stories."

"Like the world's worst missionaries."

"They're usually boys, but occasionally you'll encounter a girl." Miller scrolled his mouse wheel. "Many of these people say the black-eyed kids can communicate both aloud and telepathically. Some of these writers claim to hear the kids' voices inside their heads rather than with their ears. So, that's a difference in some stories."

As Rand listened and absorbed the information he scrubbed at a patch of dried food that had spilled onto the floor with the toe of his shoe.

"But also, those who had these experiences say that the black-eyed kids only visited them once. It seems that if the kids fail to get inside your house the first time, they give up and try someone else." Miller looked at Rand. "Do you think you're worrying too much? Maybe it was a one-off thing, and since your student didn't give them what they wanted, they'll just leave her alone."

"Hopefully. But I don't want to take any chances. I need to do something for her because…"

"You feel responsible," Miller said, as if reading his mind.

"Yes."

"I get why you feel that way, but I don't think it's true."

"The timing was too coincidental for me. I even said at the end of the lesson that once you know about the black-eyed kids, you'll have an encounter."

Miller rolled his eyes. "I know about them and they've never shown up here looking for some light reading."

Rand ignored that bit of sarcasm. "Even if they don't show up at Stacy's house again, a cleansing ceremony in her home is the least I can do. Maybe put up some wards, too. That would make both her and I feel better."

"I think that's the best thing to do," Miller said. "Also, you should probably remove them from your 'stuff-you-don't-believe-in' lecture and put them into the 'stuff-that-might-be-real' lecture."

"Maybe you're right," Rand sighed.

Miller's old computer fan whirred as he searched through more folders. An idea came to Rand.

"What if these things are coming after Stacy as a way to get to me? That's what *he* would do."

Shindael.

"When was the last time you saw him?" Miller didn't have to ask who *he* referred to.

"It's been a while. Maybe a week?" He usually paid Rand a visit at least once a day. "I know he isn't losing interest in me. He's probably waiting for something. Planning his next strike. Maybe this is it, and Stacy's the target."

Miller swiveled his chair to face his friend fully, computer forgotten. He rested his elbow on the desk. "How have you been holding up? After all that stuff that happened in Finnick? I haven't talked to you much since then."

"Good," Rand said. "As well as can be expected, I guess." His last case had been a week-long ordeal, battling the possession of a charismatic preacher in the small town of Finnick. He'd had more than one chance to surrender to Shindael and give himself up so that all others in his life could be spared. He hadn't, of course. Rand didn't make deals with demons.

"No matter what you think," Miller said, "and no matter what Shindael makes you feel, you did the right thing in fighting back. Because I'm sure that these things would have come regardless."

Rand tried to force himself to snap out of his downward spiral before it got too bad. "You're right. If they come back, I'll deal with them. This is my mission. This is what I do. If I don't, then who else will?"

"Exactly."

Rand checked his watch. "I'll head to Tessa's, and then I'll give Stacy a call and set up a time to visit her home to cleanse it."

"Why are you going to Tessa's?" Miller asked.

"Libby's supposed to stay there tonight. I have to make sure she's actually staying there. That they all are."

"Why wouldn't they? Everyone knows how you feel about Halloween."

"They do, but that doesn't mean they'll take me seriously."

Miller rose from his chair to accompany Rand to the

front of the store. The woman that had been there when Rand had arrived was still browsing the shelves.

"Oh good. She's still here," Miller whispered to Rand. "Maybe I'll actually sell something today."

"What are you up to tonight?" Rand asked.

"I'll stay up and finish some accounting. Been a while since I've done the books."

"Good man," Rand said, grabbing his friend's shoulder. "Stay inside. With this black-eyed kid thing, I have a bad feeling about Halloween this year."

"You have a bad feeling about it every year."

———

AFTER HIS FRIEND LEFT, Miller emerged from the office to find the woman waiting at the cash register. He rang up her books, making his first and likely final sale of the day. When he was alone again, he returned to his office where he eyed the box that Rand had almost opened.

Stupid, Miller chastised himself. *I should've known he'd come by. Why did I leave this out?*

He flipped open the cardboard flap and pulled out an adult XXL portable toilet Halloween costume. He'd seen it online and knew it was perfect. Miller unfolded and studied it with a smile on his face. It looked even better in person than it had on the internet.

There was no way he was missing the Boyd Street block party tonight. Rand was his good friend, sure, but the man's paranoia toward Halloween was too much.

Rand wouldn't stop Miller from hitting the biggest Halloween party in the city.

7

L ibby's mom lived with her fiancé Bill in his massive house located the city's finest, most exclusive neighborhood. The smooth roads curved alongside tranquil lakes. The houses, some of which were legitimate mansions, were spread out on generous plots of land that resembled the greens of golf courses.

"I always forget how freaking huge Bill's place is," Bailey said as they pulled up the driveway, peering out and up through the windshield. Now that school was over, she'd tied her brown hair into a loose bun and had changed into a grey, oversized t-shirt.

As much as Libby wanted to focus on the fun night ahead of her, she couldn't get Georgia's words out of her mind.

What if I do want to communicate with these spirits?

Libby had seen many terrible and frightening things, and even Georgia had experienced what these dark entities were capable of. Libby could not fathom what would drive someone to willingly step into the ring with them.

"How much space does Bill need?" Bailey asked. "Didn't he live here alone before he met your mom?"

After leaving the hospital, Libby had picked Bailey up from her house. Luckily, she didn't live far from Bill's.

"I still haven't seen every room," Libby said, pushing Georgia from her mind as they got out of her Mini Cooper, a gift from Bill. The girls took their backpacks from the trunk.

"Next time I'm here, you need to take me on the grand tour."

"Don't tell my mom, but I prefer being at my dad's. It feels more… normal." Libby used her key on the front door and they entered the high-ceilinged living room. A black, L-shaped leather couch faced a seventy-two-inch television. In front of it was a dark brown, mahogany coffee table.

"We'll set up our books and stuff here," Libby said, gesturing toward the tidy living room. *The cleaners must have come earlier,* she thought. She hated to clutter it up so soon, especially since she knew Bill liked everything spotless. But it was necessary to make the story she'd tell her dad believable.

"I still don't understand why your dad would just show up here," Bailey said. "I mean, him and your mom aren't together anymore, and she lives here with her new fiancé. It doesn't make sense."

Libby's phone chimed with a text message and she looked at the screen. It was from her dad's friend, Miller Landingham.

"Warning: your dad was just here. He's headed to Tessa's."

"Oh crap," Libby said. "My dad's on the way."

"Really?" Bailey asked.

"Yes. Quick, make this place look like it's supposed to."

Libby and Bailey opened their backpacks and spread out their books, notebooks, and pens all over the coffee table and couch. A few minutes later, the once-tidy living room looked like a full-blown study party.

Bailey stood up and examined the scene, hands on her hips. "You sure he'll fall for this? It almost looks *too* exaggerated."

"The more, the better," Libby said.

"Oh, good, you're home, Libby." Libby mother's voice came from above. Tessa stood on the landing at the top of the stairwell that looked down into the living room. She wore a black dress, striped stockings, a pointed hat—her witch costume for Bill's company's Halloween party. Makeup completely caked Tessa's face. She spread her arms and smiled. "What do you think?"

"Mom, you have change out of that *right now*," Libby said. "Dad's on the way."

Libby had already told her mom about the dance and the plan to sneak around her dad. Since Tessa was attending Bill's company's costume party that night, she and Libby had a shared interest in tricking Rand.

Tessa's face fell. "Really? How do you know?"

"Miller just texted me a heads up."

Tessa swore under her breath and retreated to her bedroom.

"She looks great," Bailey said. "What are her plans for tonight?"

"She has Bill's company's party."

Libby rubbed at her forehead. That was a close call. If her dad had shown up while her mom was in costume, the cat would've been out of the bag for sure.

"I can't imagine Bill dressing up in a costume," Bailey said as she sat down on the couch. The puffy leather cushion and back rest enveloped her.

"Mom said he wasn't planning to, since he had to host, but she convinced him to go as Frankenstein."

"Oh, I *have* to see that. Bill always seems so serious."

The front door burst open, startling Libby. Her dad spilled in and paused as he surveyed the entire room, as if investigating something. He wore dark blue jeans, a black v-neck t-shirt, and a light brown jacket.

Bailey twisted in her seat to see who had barged in. When she spotted who it was, she quickly looked away and stiffened.

"Why are you coming through the door like that?" Libby asked, exasperated. Her heart pounded from the sudden fright.

Nerves also took their hold. It was go time. Now or never. Libby's plan would either work, or her dad would figure out she was hiding something.

"This should be locked," Rand said, closing the door behind him.

Libby tried to force herself to relax and act like she had nothing to hide. "You got here fast."

"Were you expecting me?"

Libby bit her lip, realizing her mistake. "You know Mom hates it when you let yourself in."

"Anywhere my daughter lives is automatically an extension of my own home. Hey, Bailey."

Bailey raised a rigid hand in an awkward wave. She definitely looked like she was hiding something. Libby wished her friend was better under pressure.

Rand's attention went to the school supplies spread out all over the coffee table and couch. "What's all this?"

Good, Libby thought. "What's it look like?" Libby replied, hands on her hips. "We have tests coming up and we're going to study tonight."

Bailey nodded.

Her dad considered this for a moment, as if trying to detect deception. Libby maintained her poker face.

Tessa appeared at the top of the stairwell again, this time dressed in jeans and a t-shirt with her blonde hair pulled up in a bun. She glowered at Rand. "I didn't hear a knock or a doorbell."

"Anywhere my daughter lives is automatically an extension of my own home," Rand repeated.

"It's more like home invasion." Tessa came down the stairs. "What are you doing here?"

"Checking on my family," Rand said.

"You could simply call. Or text. Or do many other things that respect Bill's house and privacy."

Rand narrowed his eyes. "Have you started wearing black lipstick again?"

Libby saw it too. A dark smudge remained on the corner of her mom's lips from where she'd wiped it off too hastily and missed a spot. Tessa pivoted and walked briskly toward the kitchen.

"Don't tell me that's part of a Halloween costume," Rand said, following her.

"Are we busted?" Bailey whispered.

"Maybe Mom is," Libby said. "But I think he believes

our story." She heard her parents' voices in the kitchen, but couldn't make out what they were saying. "Hopefully we'll be fine. We'll know in a few minutes…"

TESSA GRABBED a dish towel and wetted it under the sink. She scrubbed her lips while keeping her back to Rand.

"What's going on?" Rand knew when he'd come in that something was up. He could sense it in the air. That was why he'd barged in—to give himself a better chance of catching his family unawares.

"Don't you think it's time for you lay off this whole Halloween thing?" Tessa dropped the dish towel and turned to face him. "This is getting ridiculous."

"You know it's for everyone's protection."

"We wouldn't *need* protection if you would stop doing all the crazy stuff you do."

That cut Rand deeper than he allowed himself let on. He'd spent many late nights agonizing over that very fact.

"I've been chosen for this and I can't quit. You know that." Rand began surveying the kitchen for any evidence of Halloween celebrations. He walked along the length of the counters, opening cabinets and drawers. "It wouldn't be fair to the people who need me."

"And what about *us*? How is it fair to us? Especially after your daughter went missing for *days* after your last little—what are you looking for?"

Rand opened the pantry. In Bill's massive kitchen, the pantry was twice the size of his own, but he quickly spotted the contraband on the bottom shelf—two big bags of Halloween candy. He grabbed one in each hand and held them up for Tessa to see.

She folded her arms. "The neighborhood kids are also suspended from Halloween because you say so?"

"Trick-or-treating is part of the celebration, Tessa. We've been over this."

"Bill is very active in this neighborhood community and he knows all the families. He can't just turn his porch lights off and refuse the children tonight."

Rand tore open both bags of candy and upended them into the trash can while Tessa watched.

"You've really lost it, Rand," Tessa said. "You're usually crazy, but this is going too far. Not everyone agrees with your little anti-Halloween thing."

"Just in case anyone here is planning something behind my back, I wanted to let you know that there's already been an incident."

Tessa seemed skeptical. "An incident?"

"One of my students came to me this morning and told me that last night she encountered two beings that I believe could be demonic."

"Jesus, Rand, even your students are suffering now because of you? At what point will you give it up so everyone you know can live in peace?"

Tessa had always known how to harness the guilt Rand struggled with and grind it even further. It was like his ex could read his mind and use what she found in there against him.

"Luckily, the girl did the right thing and didn't take their bait, so they left," Rand explained, sidestepping Tessa's comment. "I spoke to Miller about it. He's familiar with the beings and thinks that since she didn't fall for it, they'll just leave her alone. But still, you never know…"

"I don't want to hear any of this, Rand," Tessa said. "Stop bringing it into my life."

"I'm telling you this so you can be prepared," Rand said. "I'm just looking out for all of you."

Tessa scoffed. "If you really want to look out for us, then maybe you should move *very* far away from here."

Rand sighed and his shoulders fell. He'd also considered that particular solution. It could potentially be safer for his family, but he couldn't stand the thought of not seeing Libby regularly.

Did that make him selfish? Almost certainly. It put his desire to be in his daughter's life over her safety.

"Are you satisfied with your little checkup?" Tessa's glare had not softened after her last painful jibe. "It's time for you to go."

Rand *wasn't* satisfied, but he couldn't linger and police his family all night. He was well aware that he was getting on everyone's nerves, but it was all for their protection, whether they understood it or not. On November first, he'd chill out.

Tessa escorted him to the front door as if she were a bouncer tossing him out of a bar. Libby and Bailey sat on the couch with their textbooks and notebooks.

"Bye, girls," Rand said. "I'll text you later, Libby, to see how the studying's coming along."

"Sure," she said.

Tessa opened the door for him, but before leaving, Rand faced her again. "By the way," he said, lowering his voice. "You should totally start wearing black lipstick again. I miss those days when you wore all black and dyed your hair pink."

Tessa shoved him hard in the shoulder. "Goodbye, Rand."

"I bet Bill's never seen those pictures."

"Happy Halloween, Randolph."

She closed the door in his face.

8

The sun drifted below the horizon, leaving the sky a splotch of orange and blue. It also left a chill in the autumn air, and Stacy shivered as she rushed toward the campus library.

Inside, she found it pleasantly warm, but eerily empty. The stale smell of decades-old books was familiar and calming to her.

Although midterms were coming, no one else seemed to share her enthusiasm for studying. Or maybe everyone was preparing for the Boyd Street party that would begin later that night.

Mr. Casey had told her to go. Insisted, actually, so she wouldn't be alone. Her incident had alarmed Mr. Casey just as much as Stacy, and she'd agreed with the idea of being surrounded by people.

But first, I'll cram in a few hours of review, she thought.

She just wished the library wasn't so empty.

Stacy went to the study rooms on the second floor. Mrs. Karen was at the desk, tapping on the computer keyboard, and she looked over the tops of her glasses at Stacy when she came in.

"What are you doing here tonight?" Mrs. Karen whispered.

"The usual."

"Shouldn't you be out having fun somewhere?"

"Shouldn't you?"

Mrs. Karen only chuckled. "I'm too old for that now." She handed Stacy the sign-in book and she wrote her name. She was the only one on the page.

"All the rooms are free," Mrs. Karen said.

Stacy found her favorite, which she considered lucky. Deep down, she knew that was ridiculous, but it wasn't bad to have rituals. She unpacked her books, feeling guilty for disobeying Mr. Casey.

The study room was so quiet that when her phone rang, it scared the hell out of her. She fished it out of her pocket and checked the screen.

It was him. Mr. Casey had promised to check up on her that night.

"Hello?" Stacy felt busted—as if her teacher knew she was alone when she shouldn't be.

"Stacy. It's Rand."

"Hi, Mr. Casey."

"Just calling to make sure you're okay."

"Everything's fine so far."

"Why are you whispering?"

Stacy cleared her throat. "Sorry." She spoke normally, which sounded like screaming in the silent study room. She felt like a hypocrite—she always hated it when others answered their phones in the no-talking area of the library.

"Are you still going to the block party tonight?"

"Yes, sir."

"Good. I never tell anyone to leave the house on Halloween, but in your case you need to be with friends."

"That's my plan." Stacy glanced around the study room, feeling just how empty the place was. Perhaps she hadn't been thinking when she'd decided to study in the library. She'd never been alone in the silent study rooms before. It hadn't even occurred to her that they'd be deserted on Halloween night. Now, it seemed obvious.

"Please call me if something happens, although I don't think it will. I've spoken with someone who is familiar with the type of encounter you had, and he said because you didn't fall for their trick, they should leave you alone."

"That's good to hear," Stacy said.

"All right, Stacy. Take care."

"You too, Mr. Casey."

She hung up and placed the phone on the table.

Mr. Casey was more than just a good teacher, he was a great man, and Stacy was very thankful for him.

Although Stacy always denied it when Kim teased her, it was true Stacy had a small crush on her teacher, and him being so thoughtful during her time of need only made it worse. She wouldn't mind if he kept calling her even after the night was over.

Hopefully Mr. Casey was correct and what had happened was an isolated incident. Stacy still wasn't over it. She had barely slept the previous night.

Stacy turned to her books. Reviewing math problems would take her mind off of things.

But instead, she reached for her Intro to Supernatural Studies notebook. On the inside of the cover, she'd written two notes that Mr. Casey had told them would be the answers to questions on every test of the semester, because the information was so important.

Your authority over an evil spirit is greatest when you call them by name and command them to leave in the name of the Lord, Stacy read. She'd highlighted the note in three different colors and circled it with a marker.

The second note was equally as highlighted as the first. *Under no circumstances should you ever make a deal with any demonic entity. Although it may seem tempting, there is always a catch. Demons are masters of deception.*

True to his word, Mr. Casey had included the questions on every one of his tests and Stacy had answered each with the exact responses that she'd memorized.

Despite knowing the information by heart, she reviewed it yet again. Because if Mr. Casey was wrong and those creepy kids didn't leave her alone, then having the information memorized wouldn't be enough; she'd actually need to use it.

9

Kim's face was inches from the bathroom mirror, eyelids pulled apart, the contact lens balancing precariously on the edge of her finger.

One. Two. Three.

She placed it over her cornea and blinked away the brief discomfort as the contact settled into place. Kim didn't normally wear contact lenses, so she wasn't used to touching her own eyeball. However, her costume wouldn't be complete without them.

One down. One to go.

She did the same on the left eye, which was easier than the first. Once the tears dissipated, she checked herself in the mirror. Feline eyes looked back at her. Although painful to put in, they were the best part of her costume.

Kim's cat outfit was admittedly sparse. The pointy ears on top her of head completed the illusion, complementing the black leotard and leggings that made up the rest of her costume.

Buster, the real black cat of the house, jumped up on the toilet and inspected her.

"What do you think, Buster?" Kim asked, bringing her face close to his to show off her similar eyes. "I look just like you, don't I?"

She patted his head and ran her fingernails down his back, which he arched, as she surveyed herself in the mirror. All she had left to do was draw whiskers on her cheeks with makeup.

But first I need to figure out where Stacy is, she thought.

She picked up her phone from the side of the bathroom sink and called Stacy. It rang four times before her roommate answered.

"Hey." Stacy's voice was hushed.

"Why are you whispering?"

"I'm in the library on campus."

Kim paused for a moment. "Why are you there? I thought you were coming to Boyd Street."

"I am. But…"

"But you figured you'd study first."

"Sorry. I'm just so nervous about these tests."

Kim had been excited when Stacy had texted her at noon saying she'd changed her mind and would go with her to the block party. Kim assumed it was because of the weird experience Stacy had had the night. *She probably doesn't want to be alone on Halloween.* It was understandable, even though Kim thought Stacy was playing up whatever it was she claimed to have seen.

"Are you *really* going to come? Or are you going to study all night?"

"I'm coming."

"Well, I'm ready. Like, completely dressed. And Craig

is supposed meet me here soon."

"You go ahead," Stacy said. "I'll see you there."

"I've heard that before. Many times."

"I'm serious, Kim. I'm leaving right now." Kim heard rustling papers, closing books, and a zipping backpack. "Packing up and walking home. I'll be there in fifteen minutes."

"Do you want me and Craig to wait for you?" Kim asked.

The doorbell rang.

"No, y'all go ahead," Stacy said.

"You can't walk all the way to Boyd Street on your own," Kim said as she approached the front door. When she opened it, she was greeted by three young children dressed as a pumpkin, a ghost, and a vampire.

"Trick or treat!" they shouted in unison.

"Wow," Kim said to the group. "Cool costumes."

"You too," said the vampire. "You're a cat!"

"I am. I love cats." Kim used her shoulder to tuck the phone to her ear as she grabbed the nearby bowl of candy and dropped handfuls into the open and waiting bags.

"We have a dog," the vampire replied. "See?"

He pointed behind them. The kids' parents waited in the front yard, their black lab on a leash. They smiled and waved at Kim as she finished handing out the candy.

"What do you say?" prodded the kids' mother when the kids turned their backs.

"Thank you," they shouted back at her in unison.

Kim closed the door. "Did you hear that, Stacy? Everyone's out enjoying Halloween except for you."

"I'm glad you remembered to get candy," Stacy said. "I forgot. Anyway, don't wait up. See you soon."

They hung up. *Good. Stacy's on the way. Now, where the hell is my boyfriend?*

She dialed Craig. It rang and rang, and she thought it was about to go to voicemail when he picked up.

"Hey, baby." he shouted into the phone, though his voice was barely audible over the commotion in the background.

"Uh, *where* are you?"

"On Boyd Street."

Kim's mouth fell open. "You're not coming to get me?"

There was a long pause. "You said earlier that I should go ahead and you'd meet me."

No. What she'd said when Craig had asked if he could go early with his buddies was, "Yeah, you can if you want." She figured her annoyed tone had given off all the clues in the world as to how she really felt about that.

"So I'm just supposed to walk to Boyd Street by myself?"

"But you said—"

The doorbell rang again.

"Forget it, Craig. Stacy and I will walk together. Hope we don't get mugged and molested by axe murderers on the way."

She hung up on him. There were no axe murderers in the short distance between her house and Boyd Street, but she wanted to make Craig feel bad for not picking up on her feelings. She opened the door, and this time she had a zombie clown and a fairy dressed in a frilly pink dress.

"Trick or treat!"

"Oh, wow. You're way too scary for me," Kim told the clown. Fake blood smeared his bright-colored costume. "I think I'll have nightmares tonight."

She dumped a bunch of candy in the clown's bag as he giggled. He turned and ran off the porch back to his waiting parents, leaving his little sister. Kim crouched down to her level. "You're very pretty. Much better than that creepy clown. Here, take more." She scooped three handfuls into the girl's bag, and the child beamed.

It was imperative that Kim have no candy remaining in the house after the night was over—she didn't pay for gym classes four times a week just to have her hard work undone. "Promise you won't tell him?"

"I promise," the fairy said, elated at their little conspiracy.

"Good. Have a happy Halloween."

"Thank you."

She returned to her parents, and Kim waved at them before closing the door behind her.

Right. Where was I?

The whiskers. She'd draw those on, have a beer, and wait for Stacy to arrive. Now that she was pissed at Craig, there was no reason to rush.

The doorbell rang again.

Ugh. I need to turn off the porch lights. I'll never finish getting ready with all these interruptions.

She opened the door. Two young boys stood side-by-side.

"Happy Halloween," she said, reaching for the bowl of candy. When she turned back to them, she saw that neither of them wore a costume. Only simple, dirty clothes and, oddly, no shoes.

"What are you two supposed to be?" she asked.

Neither responded. They stared ahead, past her and into the house.

"No costumes, huh? I like your style. Skip the hard work and go straight for the candy." Kim glanced over their heads, but found no parents in the yard.

In fact, everything was now much quieter than it had been when she'd opened the door a minute before. The groups of trick-or-treaters that had filled the sidewalks had all gone away.

"How did you convince your parents to let you out without them?" No response.

Whatever.

"Here you go." She lowered the bowl. "Take however much you want." Neither of them carried a bag to collect their candy. "No candy? Fine. Have a happy Halloween." She went to close the door.

"We need to come in and use your telephone," the older of the two boys said.

Kim froze. "You both were here last night, weren't you?" Neither responded. "You met my friend Stacy. You asked her the same question."

"We just need to come in and use your telephone," the older boy said. "We aren't bad people. We aren't going to hurt you."

Something was very off-putting about the way he spoke. He sounded so *proper* for such a young kid.

Kim set the bowl of candy down. "You scared my friend pretty badly last night."

"We're sorry." His response was flat and emotionless, like reading a line off a cue card.

"Doesn't seem so, but whatever. Look, she'll be here in a few minutes. Why don't you come in? You can apologize to her when she gets here."

The two boys stepped inside.

10

They walked evenly side-by-side, stiff and rigid as if wearing a back brace. Kim watched them as they turned into the kitchen.

Weirdos, she thought.

She closed the front door. At least Stacy could see that they were harmless and that there was nothing for her to be afraid of. Then Kim would kick them out, head to the party, and have a good night.

When Kim returned to the kitchen, she found the boys sitting at the table, looking into their laps. Their shaggy, greasy hair hung low over their foreheads. They must have been siblings, although not twins—the one that had spoken was older than the other. But all their movements were in unison.

"Well, make yourself at home, why don't you?" No response. "You two aren't staying for long. You're just here to apologize to my friend, then you're out. I'm not babysitting tonight."

She picked up her eyeliner from where she'd left it on

the kitchen table and used the magnetized mirror on the refrigerator door to draw whiskers on her cheeks.

"I don't know why you're wasting your Halloween. Soon you'll be too old to go trick-or-treating."

She finished her last whisker and glanced at them in the mirror. They were both looking at her.

Kim turned to face them, but when she did, she found them looking down again.

"Hopefully you'll be less shy when you grow up. Do you want something to drink?"

She opened the fridge and grabbed a can of beer and it hissed as she pulled the tab. She took a sip. "You can't have this, but I have water. I might also have some juice. Wait, forget it. It's expired."

Kim took the bottle of juice and carried it to the sink. She poured it out and threw the bottle in the trash. She leaned on the counter, tapped Stacy's name in the recent calls list and brought the phone to her ear. "Do you still need to use my phone? I'll let you after I call my friend."

"Hey, I'm almost there," Stacy said when she answered.

"Good. Because we have visitors."

"Craig and his friend? I told you, I'm not interested in Steve."

"I know you're not interested in Steve. You're too obsessed with your ghost teacher. But there are two other young gentlemen who want to meet you."

"What do you mean? Who?"

A grotesque smell filled Kim's nostrils, and she coughed. It smelled like a combination of sulfur and feces.

"Jesus," she said, pushing herself from the counter. She walked into the living room to get away from the stench.

Aren't they too old to shit their pants?

"Jesus?"

"No him. It's the two boys from last night. They came back."

There was a long silence on the other end of the phone.

"Hello?"

"The kids with black eyes?" Stacy said, almost too low to hear.

Kim realized she hadn't actually made eye contact with them yet. They seemed to avoid it. "I don't think so. But they're barefoot, and they asked to use my telephone. Just like you said."

"Oh my God," Stacy said.

"Relax. They're fine."

"What do you mean?"

Something moved in Kim's periphery—Buster. The black cat emerged from the hallway and walked into the living room. He peeked around the corner and spotted the two boys at the kitchen table. He hissed loudly. His back arched, his hair rose, and he opened his mouth to display his fangs.

"Buster," Kim shouted.

Buster only turned tail and sprinted down the hallway, meowing as he went.

"Kim, what do you mean they're fine?" Stacy asked again. "You told them to leave, didn't you?"

"No. They're sitting right here in the kitchen."

Kim flipped the light on in the hallway, looking for where Buster had run off to. Something had really pissed him off.

"Kim, you have to get out of there." Stacy sounded so serious that it was almost funny.

"Relax. I brought them in here to make them apologize to you for scaring you."

"Leave the house *right now*."

Kim rolled her eyes. "Stacy, come on." She turned the light off in the hall and went back to the living room. "You can't seriously—"

When Kim looked into the kitchen, she noticed the two boys had gotten up from the table and were standing side-by-side, just as they had been on the porch.

Underneath their shaggy hair were eyes blacker than the darkest night. Four voids that seemed to compel her to stare back.

"Kim. I'm serious. You need to leave."

Stacy's voice was distant now. The connection on the line turned to garbled static.

Kim wanted to move, to look away, but her body felt as if trapped in a block of ice. Her fingers loosened and the phone fell from her palm, clattering on the hardwood floor.

The two boys gave her a ghastly smile.

11

Stacy Thompson had never run so fast in her life. She sprinted down the sidewalk, her heavy, full backpack bouncing up and down.

She kept her phone to her ear as she ran. "Kim. You need to get out there."

No response. She checked the screen and saw that the line had disconnected. She called back.

It rang and rang.

"Hey. This is Kim. Sorry I missed your call, but if you —" Stacy hung up and called again.

Pick up, Kim!

She turned the corner into the neighborhood and tore down the sidewalk, feet landing heavily on the cracked and uneven concrete. She darted around families of trick-or-treaters who looked at her strangely as she zipped past them.

The front door of her house was open. She bounded up the steps.

All the lights were on and everything was silent and

still. The only sound was the buzzing of Kim's phone on the floor.

Stacy hung up and Kim's phone stopped buzzing. It lay in a puddle of beer, the can nearby and on its side.

"Kim?"

Stacy's pulse pounded in her ears.

The kitchen was empty. The room smelled terribly, and there was a black fluid smeared all over the floor.

She turned on the light in the hallway. Nothing. Only the door at the end of the hall—her bedroom—was open.

Stacy didn't want to be there. What if the black-eyed kids were hiding somewhere inside?

"Kim, where are you?"

Stacy crept forward, and the aged hardwood floor creaked beneath her feet. She went into her bedroom and heard meowing underneath her bed. Stacy got down and saw Buster curled in a ball. His green eyes were wide and his entire body was shaking.

Stacy straightened and checked Kim's room and the bathroom, but she was nowhere to be found. The house was empty.

Tears formed as her mind raced with all kinds of thoughts and possibilities.

I need to call the police.

She lifted her phone, but wondered what she would say. That her friend let in two kids with black eyes, and now she was missing?

The dispatcher answered. "Nine-one-one, what's your emergency?"

"My roommate is missing and I think she was taken."

"Where was her last known location?"

Stacy gave her address.

"I'll send an officer. Where are you now?"

"I'm here at my house."

"Are you alone in the home?"

"No one's here. I checked."

"Good. Please remain calm until someone arrives."

Stacy hung up on the dispatcher and immediately called Mr. Casey.

12

R and slid his fingers between the blinds and spread them apart. His neighborhood was usually quiet at that hour, but there were still some families and their costumed children going door to door, trick-or-treating.

Mrs. Blatch, who lived across the street, was posted up on a lawn chair in her yard with a big bowl of candy in her lap. As long as Rand had lived there, Mrs. Blatch had always been enthusiastic about Halloween.

A pair of kids started up Rand's driveway. Before they got too far, their parents shouted after them and gestured for them to move along. The kids sulked back to the road where they continued on to the next house. Rand's porch lights were off, as they always were on Halloween night. No trick-or-treaters welcome.

Rand turned away from the window. On the coffee table, Rand's large, leather-bound Bible lay open from when he'd tried reading it earlier. It beckoned to him now, drawing his gaze. He forced himself to sit on the couch and lean toward it. But still he felt disconnected.

Rand always spent Halloween reading his Bible and praying. He drew comfort from its holy words and the powerful promises of God to save mankind from the clutches of hell.

But this Halloween seemed darker than the ones before. This year, Rand found that the Scriptures no longer shed the hopeful light that it once had.

His Bible was open to the first page of the book of Job. Rand related to the story a bit too well. In it, God allowed Satan to test Job, a faithful man, by afflicting him with a series of horrible misfortunes. In the end, Job stood strong and his faith in God never faltered.

That night, though, Rand couldn't even get through the first paragraph. He could no longer claim to be like Job. Rand had failed his test of faith.

When Rand looked at the heavy tome that contained the words of God, he couldn't help but remember his previous case. Deckard Arcan, a false preacher that was possessed by a demon from hell, had been leading all the faithful in the small town of Finnick down a dark path. At least he had been until Rand stopped Deckard and banished the demon back to hell.

That case had tested Rand more than any other had before. Rand had mustered all of his faith and hope that God would finally intervene on his behalf and help him in the spiritual battle.

Yet God had been silent.

Rand had barely escaped from that demonic battle with his life. He'd only survived because of help from his friend Miller and an old preacher named Simon. Since that point, Rand had struggled to trust God for anything. Here he was, fighting on the front lines against the devil's servants, risking his life and family, without a single sign that God was grateful.

Rand bowed his head and closed his eyes and clasped his hands together between his knees.

God, he prayed. *On this evil night, please protect my—*

He found himself unable to go any further. It must've been his tenth failed attempt at prayer that night. If he'd learned anything from his last case, it was that he was alone in the fight against evil. God had no intention on making himself known.

Rand was the only one who was going to lift a finger to protect his family and fight for his clients. Even though Rand was doing what he thought would have been God's job, the creator of the universe remained silent and distant.

But Rand had pulled through without God's help on his last case. He figured he'd probably have to do it again on his next. That was the reason he drove his family crazy with his overprotection on Halloween—because he was only one man and he could only do so much if something went wrong.

God could not be counted on.

Rand turned away from his Bible and leaned back on his couch. He drummed his fingers on his thighs. The pattering of them hitting his jeans was the only sound in his deathly silent house.

It's too quiet, he thought. He was starting to feel like he was inside of a tomb.

Rand picked up the remote and turned the television. He scanned the channels, but everything showing was related to Halloween: zombies, slashers, monster movies. One station was even having a twenty-four-hour marathon of *The Exorcist*.

Definitely not watching that, Rand thought. *That movie isn't fictional.*

He ended up leaving the TV on the weather radar.

Rand got up from the couch and went to his bedroom. He'd already changed the bed sheets and vacuumed the carpet. His nervous energy had made him quite productive. Rand opened his top drawer and started matching his socks. He swore that after a long enough period of time, socks took on a natural fit to his left or right foot. He liked to pair them accordingly.

Tomorrow morning couldn't come soon enough.

Rand's cell phone rang, causing a jolt of anxiety. He rushed to where he'd left it on the coffee table in the living room, next to his Bible.

It was Libby. His heart sank.

"Libby, is everything okay?"

"Relax, Dad. Jeez."

"You're okay?"

"Yes. I'm checking on you. Clearly you're the one who's not okay."

Rand took in a quick deep breath and lit out, settling himself. "You can't scare me like that."

"How? By calling? You need to chill."

"You know how I feel about tonight."

"Yeah, which is why I'm seeing if you're all right."

Rand dropped onto the couch. His legs had grown weak and rubbery. "As good as can be expected." *Even if I am a little anxious,* he thought. "What are you doing?"

"Bailey and I are taking a study break. Watching a horror movie."

"Which one?" he asked, hoping to catch her off guard if she was lying.

"*Halloween II*," she answered without hesitation.

Rand snatched up the remote control and brought up the menu on his television. He jumped to the movie channels and scrolled. Sure enough, *Halloween II* was beginning.

"You still there?" Libby asked.

"Yeah. Do you and Bailey need anything?"

"Only for you to relax and take a load off. You're stressing me out."

"I'll try. Be good and stay indoors."

"Right."

Rand could practically hear her rolling her eyes through the phone. "Where's your mother?"

"Upstairs. Or in the back. Somewhere in this huge house."

"But she's home?"

"Yes, Dad," Libby droned. "Her and Bill are both here."

"Maybe I'll call her."

"Don't you think you've annoyed her enough for one day?"

Probably, he thought.

"Call me if you need me," Rand said.

"I'd say the same, but you're starting to irritate me. Good night, Dad."

"Night."

Rand dropped the phone onto the couch near his thigh.

A few seconds later, the phone rang, and once again

the sound startled him. He figured it was just Libby calling again about something she'd forgotten to mention.

But when Rand checked the screen, he saw it was Stacy Thompson. His other hand gripped the couch cushion. "Oh no."

He straightened, his entire body sick with worry.

Rand brought the phone to his ear. "Hey Stacy. Are you—"

"Mr. Casey. She's gone," Stacy replied, sounding hysterical.

Rand shot to his feet. "Stacy, what's going on?"

Stacy rambled on, but she was crying too hard and nothing she said was clear.

"Stacy. Try to calm down. I can't understand anything you're saying."

She took several frantic breaths, making the line sound like static. "Mr. Casey, she's gone, Kim's *gone*. Disappeared. She let the kids in and now she's *gone*."

There were other incoherent words thrown in between the sobs, but Rand had heard what he needed to.

"Stacy," Rand said. "Where are you right now?"

"I'm at home and Kim's missing."

Rand remembered that Kim was Stacy's roommate. She'd been there when Stacy had first encountered the black-eyed kids.

"When did you discover she was missing?" Rand strived to keep calm.

"Just a few minutes ago. She called and said she let the kids in, and I told her to leave but she wouldn't believe me and then I ran back here but I wasn't fast enough and now she's gone."

Someone finally let them in, Rand thought. He remembered the conversation he'd had with Miller earlier.

No one knew what happened once you let them in.

Rand could only hope that Kim had run away. Hiding at a neighbor's house or something.

"Mr. Casey!" Stacy shouted; he'd been silent too long.

"Okay. I'm coming over. Send me a pin of your location."

"Are you coming now? I don't know what to do. I called the police, but I don't know what—"

"Whoa," Rand interrupted. "Stacy, listen to me. Call the police back right now and tell them *not* to come."

Stacy was silent for a moment, probably wondering if she'd heard correctly. "What?"

"Yes. Call them back and tell them not to come."

"But I already told them that my roommate was missing."

"Tell them it was a bad Halloween prank and she's there and everything's fine."

In cases where the supernatural were concerned, calling the police only made things worse. Rand had learned that lesson the hard way several years ago. Cops investigated their cases with logic and deductive reasoning. That was a good thing, to be sure, but it simply wasn't the best solution in supernatural situations.

"Are you sure?" Stacy asked.

"Yes. Do it. Then send me a pin of your location. I'm heading to my car now."

"Okay…"

"Stay put. I'm coming."

"You promise?"

"Yes. I am already on the way."

13

Although Libby had played countless volleyball games inside the high school gymnasium, that night she hadn't recognized it all when she'd arrived. It had completely transformed. Heavy beats boomed as a DJ played songs at the front of the gym. Strobe lights flashed a wide array of colors around the room. The costumed students congregated either on the dance floor or off to the sides in groups.

Now, Libby was near the speakers, dancing close with Parker Haney, who was dressed like a giant deer. Libby wore a camouflage hunting outfit, complete with an orange vest and a bow. When she and Parker had gone to take their picture, Vicky Stuart had told them she was entering them as finalists for the costume contest.

As they danced, Libby remembered to check on her friend. She spotted Bailey and Terrance, both wearing matching skeleton costumes, standing near the wall and chatting. As usual, Bailey was doing all the gabbing while Terrance stood there, nervous and nodding along.

Libby felt Parker's hands slide too low down her backside. *Time for a break,* she thought. She leaned back and shouted in his ear, "I'm going to check on them."

Parker glanced over to Bailey and Terrance. "They're fine. Let them be."

Libby pulled out of Parker's arms and shouldered her way out of the circle of dancing students. As she distanced herself from the speakers, her eardrums rang, muffling all other sounds besides the music.

"Libby," Bailey said when she saw Libby approach. "Terrance just told me he wants to study abroad in Italy for a semester in college. Haven't I always talked about wanting to do that too?"

"Yeah, you won't shut up about it, actually," Libby said, casting Terrance a small smile. He still seemed awkward and tense around them.

"It's *muy bene*," Bailey said.

"Excuse me," Terrance said. "I need to use the bathroom. I'll be right back." He left them alone.

"Do you think he's having fun?" Bailey asked as she watched him go. "This doesn't seem like his thing."

"I've noticed you doing all the talking. Maybe he has something to say, but he's just waiting for you to zip it."

Bailey shrugged. "Wouldn't surprise me. He's a really interesting dude. I can't believe I've never really had a conversation with him before now. His dad flies airplanes and is teaching him how. They go up almost every weekend and he promised to take me sometime. Isn't that cool?"

"That *is* pretty neat," Libby said.

"How are things going with Mr. Swim Team?"

"Even dressed as a deer he's super-hot." Libby looked

back to where they'd been dancing, but he wasn't there anymore.

"Tell me about it," Bailey said.

Libby scanned the gym until she found Parker again. He was with two of his friends and they were talking amongst themselves.

"Have you checked in with your dad?" Bailey asked.

"Only once before we left," Libby said. "I haven't since then, and probably won't again tonight. I don't want to overdo it, you know? He sounded reassured when we talked, so I think he'll be fine until morning."

"So we'll get away with this after all."

"Looks that way. Thank God. It's good to finally spend Halloween like a normal person."

She hated having to lie to her dad, but now that it was all said and done, she was enjoying herself.

Nothing bad has happened at all, she thought. *All that drama for what?*

Parker Haney left his friends and crossed the dance floor to where Bailey and Libby stood. The big antlers of his costume protruded to either side of his head.

"You all right?" Parker asked.

"All good," Libby said.

"Excellent. So listen…" He licked his lips. "Me and the boys are thinking we should get out of here."

That took Libby by surprise. "Oh."

"I mean all of us," Parker added. "As a group. Us three and them. And Terrance."

To Libby, this sounded like it had been Parker's plan before they'd even arrived at the Halloween dance, and she wished Parker had mentioned it. "And go where, exactly?"

Parker hesitated a second before answering. "The Boyd Street block party."

"Oh my gosh *yes!*" Bailey shouted.

"No way," Libby said.

Bailey and Parker looked at her.

"What's wrong?" Parker asked.

"Yeah," Bailey said. "What's the deal?"

"You guys can go if you want. I'm not."

"Why not?"

"Too risky."

"Risky how?" Bailey said. "Do you mean your dad? You told me it was a done deal. All obstacles avoided."

"Still. Just coming here is pushing my luck. I know if I try to do too much, then I'll get found out."

"Is your old man at the block party?" Parker asked.

"No."

"Where is he right now?"

"Home."

"Exactly," Parker said. Libby hated that he'd led her down his trap. "He's home for the night. There's no way he'll find out."

"Well, what if one of his students sees me? It's a college thing."

"Do they know what you look like?" Bailey asked.

I'm going to thrash her later for taking Parker's side on this, Libby thought. "I've been to his class once or twice."

"They'll recognize you at night, in a huge crowd, *and* in costume?" Parker flashed his charming smile. "Not buying it."

Libby sighed. She knew her arguments weren't holding a lot of water, but there was no other way to explain the bad gut feeling she had toward the idea. She could fool her dad for a little while, but he was always crafty enough to eventually figure it out.

"She's got no other excuses," Bailey said. "I think that means she's in."

Terrance rejoined them from the bathroom. He glanced at each of them in turn as they stood in silence. "What's going on?"

"How does the Boyd Street block party sound?" Bailey asked him.

Terrance seemed surprised. "Uh… sure?"

"Good man." Bailey punched his arm playfully, and Terrace recoiled. "You see, Libby? That's three against one. You're outvoted."

Libby was *definitely* going to give her friend an earful about this in the morning. Bailey knew how risky it was, but Boyd Street was just the kind of thing Bailey would be into—she couldn't wait to go to college and was always angling to get invites to parties.

Libby sighed. *Dad should be asleep. Maybe I* am *being paranoid.*

"In that case, who's driving?"

14

Soon after Rand left, his phone chimed with a text—Stacy's location. He put it into his phone's GPS and sped along, hoping to not pass any police officers on the way.

Fifteen minutes later, Rand almost put his Jeep on two wheels as he turned into Stacy's neighborhood while barely braking. The sides of the narrow streets were filled with the residents' parked cars, leaving no space for Rand's. So, Rand parked his car in the middle of the road in front of Stacy's house and bolted out.

He stopped short. Rand saw Stacy sitting on her front porch steps, knees pulled up to her chest and face buried into her jeans. The front door was wide open behind her.

His heart broke for her. *This is all my fault*, he thought. Rand wished these ghosts and demons would only come after him. But they knew the best way to harm him was to target the other people in his life.

Stacy looked up as he approached. Her eyes were puffy and face red, streaked from her tears. She stood up and threw her arms around Rand's neck in a tight hug, and then she pulled away from him just as suddenly. "Sorry. I'm just…"

"It's okay," Rand said. "Let's sit back down."

Rand sat down with Stacy on the top porch step.

"I didn't know what else to do, so I called you," Stacy said.

"You did the right thing. Did you call the police back?" She nodded. "Any problems?"

She wiped her nose and sniffled. "They asked if I was sure everything was okay, and I said yes. They said they'll cancel their dispatch and told me to tell my friends that pranks like that aren't funny on Halloween."

"Okay, good."

"But Mr. Casey. If… something's happened to Kim, why can't we call the police?"

"You're just going to have to trust me on that one," Rand said. "When supernatural stuff happens, the cops always make things worse. Now, I want to hear your story."

Stacy looked away as she recollected. "Well, I was at the library on campus… I know you told me to go to Boyd Street, and I swear I was going to, but I wanted to get some studying in before I did. Anyway, I was on the way home and Kim called me and said…" She swallowed. "That *they* had come back and she'd let them in. I tried to tell her to get out of the house but the call disconnected. And when I got back, she was gone."

As Rand listened, his dread grew. He had a serious problem on his hands. Stacy looked at him with new tears glistening in her eyes. "Can you help me? Can you help Kim?"

"Yes, I can," Rand said. "First, though, I'll take a look around."

He rose and walked into the house, stepping carefully like a detective at a crime scene wary of spoiling any evidence. A cell phone—Kim's, he presumed—lay on the floor in the living room in a puddle of spilled beer. The can was nearby, indicating that she'd dropped both at the same time.

The house smelled awful, like a combination of sulfur and animal feces. That lingering stench, he knew, was from the entities. There was black residue on the floor in the kitchen and living room. Rand followed it, making sure not to step in it, and found puddles of the same stuff on two of the four chairs at the kitchen table.

They sat here, he thought.

He pictured the black-eyed kids coming in and taking a seat while Kim spoke to Stacy on the phone. At some point, they must have attacked her and taken her away.

Rand went down the hallway and checked the bedrooms and bathroom, but everything seemed normal. All the action had occurred in the living room and kitchen.

When he returned to the living room, he saw Stacy had come back inside. Her arms were folded and she looked worried. "Well?"

Rand crouched down next to the black stuff puddled on the hardwood floor. It had the consistency of muddy rainwater that had been tracked in on the bottom of dirty shoes. He dipped his finger into it and rubbed it between the pads of his thumb and forefinger, then sniffed it shorty, the horrific odor assaulting him.

"This is where the smell is coming from."

"Plasma," Stacy said. Rand eyed her. "The stuff left behind by demons. You taught us about it in class."

"That's right," Rand said.

"It's not anything that will ever be found naturally on Earth," Stacy continued. "It's an entirely new substance from another world." She rattled off the information as if it were common knowledge. The girl had studied for his class so much that, by now, these facts about dark entities probably *were* common knowledge to her.

"Precisely," Rand said, standing.

"So these two kids *are* demons."

"It seems so. The way they appear and disappear, as well as the smell and plasma they leave behind."

"The black eyes," Stacy added.

"That also."

"You taught us that they can't take on a complete human form. There will always be a flaw in their disguise. For these kids, the flaw is their eyes."

"Correct."

Stacy chewed her lip as she looked around the room. "And what about Kim?" She appeared sick with worry.

Rand realized what Stacy was asking. *No blood. No body. No signs of injury.*

"I don't believe they've hurt her," Rand said. "I think they've only taken her."

"If that's the case… taken her where?"

"That's what I need to figure out."

Although Rand was trying his best to maintain the appearance of the stalwart professional, he knew he was treading into unknown waters with this one. He'd cleansed haunted houses. He'd guided lost spirits to the afterlife. He'd cast out demons from possessed people. But up until that morning when Stacy had told him her story, Rand had believed the black-eyed kids to be nothing more than an urban legend. He didn't know what these entities wanted, and he didn't know what they were capable of.

Rand remembered the Bible he'd left open to the book of Job on his coffee table. It seemed the black-eyed kids would be yet another deadly test dropped on Rand's shoulders. And he was already sure that God would remain silent the entire time.

Regardless, Stacy needed his help. He had to push forward with or without God's support. He had to figure out how to get Kim back from the black-eyed kids.

Rand followed the trail of plasma outside and onto the porch. He spotted something on the concrete path leading up to Stacy's house. "Do you have a flashlight?"

Stacy opened the drawer near the door and pulled out a long, black flashlight. She clicked it on to see if it still worked, and when it lit up she handed it to Rand. He shined the beam on the ground. The residue left behind by the black-eyed kids was less concentrated there, but now that he scrutinized it with a light, he saw that there was something else.

"Did you touch any of this stuff?" he asked Stacy over his shoulder.

"No. I stepped over it." Stacy joined Rand and studied the sludge alongside him.

"Do you see what I see?" Rand asked.

"It looks like a child's footprint. Wait, there's two feet." She pointed toward the sidewalk where there were, in fact, two sets of footprints. Two sets of *left* footprints.

"Both of them were barefoot when I saw them," Stacy said.

"Demonic entities leave footprints behind sometimes, but they tend to only be left-sided footprints," Rand said.

"Because left is associated with things that are backwards, wrong, and evil?" Stacy recited.

"Correct," Rand said, impressed.

The footprints led all the way to the street and then turned left where they continued down the sidewalk. But the direction of the footprints indicated that the kids had walked *toward* Stacy's house, not away.

"These were made before they arrived at my house," Stacy said. "They came from that direction." She pointed down the street, to the left. "Which means…"

Rand and Stacy looked at each other as the thought dawned on them at the same time.

"Your house wasn't the first place they visited tonight," Rand said.

15

The group returned to Parker's car, where he removed his deer head and put it in the trunk so he could fit inside. Libby got into the passenger seat and the two skeletons climbed into the back.

"I'm glad you came around," Parker said as he started the ignition. "Where we're going will be way better than a school dance."

"We were finalists for the costume contest, you know," Libby told him.

Parker fished a small hip flask out of the center console. He unscrewed the top and went to take a sip, but Libby swiped it out of his hands before it reached his lips.

"Hey," he said.

"Just drive. Save this for later."

Parker gave her mock puppy eyes, but she only pointed ahead. "Come on." She screwed the lid back onto the flask and tucked it into the breast pocket of her camo shirt.

Parker drove fast and reckless toward the university.

Boyd Street was adjacent to campus, and many college students lived in the area, which was why it had become such a popular spot for the huge Halloween party over the years. Libby had never been, but she'd heard about it, and figured she'd try it out if she stayed in state for college. She still had her reservations about going there, but as she rode along, listening to Parker's loud music and holding on when he took sharp turns, she realized that maybe she was being overly cautious.

"Ah, crap," Parker said after he turned onto one of the narrow neighborhood roads. Cars lined the street on both sides and throngs of pedestrians in costumes blocked the way forward.

He inched behind them, but they made no effort to get out of his way. Many of them held drinks, and some of them even swayed. Parker flashed his brights at them, but a guy dressed as a caveman only gave him the finger.

"Are we here?" Libby asked. She didn't know her way around the neighborhoods near campus.

"We're five blocks away," Parker said, "and already it's packed."

"We have to park and walk like everyone else," Bailey said.

Parker groaned. He swerved into an empty space between two cars, parallel parking with surprising swiftness. He leaned over the console and gave Libby a big, goofy grin. "I got us here in one piece. *Now* can I have my flask for the long hike in?"

"How are you planning to drive us home?" Libby said.

"You're a stickler for the rules, I see." He flashed his smile and then threw open his door.

Libby got out and slung her hunting bow over her back, while Parker collected his antlers from the trunk.

"Do you mean five long blocks or five short blocks?" Bailey asked.

"Either way, you're here now," Parker said. "May as well put in the leg work and have a good time."

Bailey looked at Terrance. "You okay with walking?" He shrugged.

Seems like Terrance just goes with the flow, Libby thought.

Parker opened a text on his phone. "Ah. My friends are already on Boyd Street." Since Parker's car didn't have enough room for everyone, his friends had ridden with someone else. "We'll meet up with them."

The group started the trek, and Libby was immediately thankful her costume had called for comfortable boots. Her thick camo hunting shirt and pants also kept her warm in the chilly night.

She pulled her phone from her pocket and checked. It was nine-thirty and there was no message from her dad.

"I heard that last year the cops had to shut this down because some guy drank too much and ran around naked," Parker said. "When they arrested him, he kept saying it was part of his costume."

"I heard that story," Bailey said, "but I think it was just a rumor."

"Oh, maybe." Parker shrugged. "It's still funny, though."

"What about you?" Libby asked him. "How do you act when you're drunk?"

"Give me my flask and find out."

"I think I'd rather not."

"Maybe you should," Bailey said. "If there are cops here and they catch you with it, you'll get an MIP."

Minor in possession. Libby hadn't considered that.

"Good point, Bailey," Parker said. "Lib, feel free to hang onto it for me."

"Ha," Libby said. "Here, you—"

They walked by two young boys standing side-by-side near the sidewalk. Libby had not seen them at first, and it was like they had appeared from nowhere. They stood unmoving, staring straight ahead, and seemed to blend in with the night.

One wore a filthy red-and-white striped t-shirt and blue shorts, the other a black shirt and shorts. Both had shaggy hair and, for some reason, they were barefoot, even though it was chilly.

Libby and her three friends fell silent as they passed.

Something about them gave Libby the creeps and she wanted to get away as quickly as possible. Once they were past the kids, the other three burst out laughing.

"That was awkward," Bailey said.

"Did anyone even see where they came from?" Parker asked.

"No. It was like they just suddenly appeared.."

"Creepy as hell."

Libby didn't find it funny. She'd felt something very off about them.

"I'll go back and invite them to the party," Parker said.

"Shut up," Bailey told him. "They were like five years old."

"Nah. Maybe nine or ten. I might just ask them to hold my flask for me. The cops wouldn't get them in trouble—"

"Uh, guys." Terrance spoke up for the first time since they'd left the car.

Libby turned and followed Terrance's gaze as he

looked behind them. The two boys were on the sidewalk, looking at them, and about ten paces away.

"Are they following us?" Bailey whispered.

Libby watched them back. She didn't like the way they stood so still, or how they seemed to extend from the darkness that surrounded them. Her gut told her to get as far from them as possible.

Parker pushed between Bailey and Terrance and shouted at them. "Hey. Why don't you two fuck off?"

Bailey shoved him. "Parker. They're just kids."

The kids said nothing. Nor did they move.

"Come on," Parker told them.

They started walking again.

"You can't curse at kids like that," Bailey said.

"Why not?"

"Because they'll pick it up and start saying it."

"I'm sure they've heard their mom and dad say worse. I mean, they must have crappy parents. Who lets their kids wander around by themselves at this time of night on Halloween?"

"Guys," Terrance said again.

They all halted and looked behind them. The kids were still the same distance away as they had been the last time they'd paused.

Parker straightened and went to shout at them again, but Bailey only put her hand on his shoulder and stopped him.

"Are y'all okay?" she asked them, concerned.

"We need you to take us to your house," answered one of the kids. It was so dark that Libby couldn't see which of the two had spoken.

"Our house?" Parker whispered.

"We… don't live around here," Bailey said. "Where are your parents?"

"Please," the kid said, louder. "We need you take us to your house. Now."

"Guys, they aren't wearing shoes," Terrance said.

Libby glanced at their feet. Terrance was right. In fact, they were only wearing shorts and t-shirts. It was way too cold to be dressed like that.

"Something's wrong," Libby said, although it was barely more than a whisper, and no one paid her any attention.

"I said we don't live near here," Bailey said. "But you can use my phone to call your parents."

"Why won't you listen to me?" the kid shouted, causing Bailey to flinch. "We just need you to take us to your house. We aren't going to hurt you."

Libby didn't like the way they were talking. It wasn't normal—their diction was too precise, their movements too still and not like children at all. "Guys." She grabbed Bailey's and Parker's arms. "We have to go."

"We have to help them," Terrance said. "They're alone out here."

Libby froze when the shorter of the two boys looked right at her. She knew he was because she could *feel* his gaze pierce through her. A heaviness of despair washed over her, and for the first time, she saw that his eyes were completely black. They were like portals that sucked her in.

'You know he isn't real, don't you?'

Libby heard the voice in her head. It was a dark, gleeful voice that delighted in her fear.

She knew the voice had come from those kids,

speaking telepathically. And if they were speaking telepathically, then they were not of this world.

She and her friends had to get away from them.

"Come on." Libby pulled her friends along as she turned and ran. The others were so startled by her reaction that they didn't think, and only ran with her.

"Where are we going?" Terrance shouted from the back of the group. "What about the kids?"

They bounded down the street, turning left and zipping between the parked cars along the side of the road. Libby was in front, but didn't even know if she was heading in the right direction toward Boyd Street. She didn't care. All she knew was she had to get away from those kids.

"I can't run anymore," Terrance called.

Although Libby had the stamina to keep going, she slowed and stopped. The other three gasped for breath.

Libby looked behind them, then all around. The kids had not followed.

"What was that?" Bailey said to Libby, almost angry. "What if they needed us?"

"They didn't, Bailey. I got a terrible feeling from them."

"A bad feeling?" Terrance said. "They were only kids."

"They weren't," Libby said. Her pulse felt as if pounding through her entire body, not only from the sudden sprinting, but also from the fear.

"What does that mean?" Terrance asked.

Libby looked at Bailey. "It was a *really* bad feeling. Do you know what I'm saying?"

"You mean…"

"Yeah."

She put her hand on her forehead, eyes wide. "Just like that? Walking along the side of the road?"

"What are you two talking about?" Parker asked.

"Come on," Libby said. "Let's keep moving."

"I'm going back," Terrance said. "They're in trouble." He walked away from the group.

"Terrance, wait," Bailey called.

"Let him go," Libby said. "They won't be there when he gets there."

"How do you know?" Parker asked.

Libby didn't respond.

They waited several minutes until Terrance returned. When he came back, he only shrugged. "They're gone."

They walked in silence the rest of the way toward the block party. All Libby could think about was how she wanted to go home. She also knew she should call her dad and tell him what she'd seen. But that would mean getting into loads of trouble.

Dad was right, she thought. *I ended up having an encounter.*

She prayed she could go the rest of the night without another.

"What was all that about?" Parker asked.

Libby really didn't want to get into it. Bailey had understood her, but Bailey knew a lot more about her than Parker did.

"I'll explain it to you later," she said.

"What's wrong with now?"

Libby dug the flask from her pocket and handed it to Parker. He took it from her, and that seemed to placate him. He unscrewed the top and took a long swig.

16

"Your house was not the first place they visited tonight," Rand said.

Stacy looked as if she wanted to shrivel up into a little ball. "What do we do?"

"Let's see where these tracks lead," Rand said. He had to make sure everyone else on the block was all right.

Rand began following the black footprints along the sidewalk—two left feet with the small stride of a young child—while Stacy reluctantly stayed one step behind. Rand swept the flashlight beam over the path, making sure to not lose the trail.

They took a sharp left and turned up the walkway toward Stacy's neighbor's front door. The tracks led to the porch.

"Looks like they were ringing a few different doorbells tonight." He glanced at Stacy, who looked at the line of footprints with a worried expression. She kept her arms folded across her stomach and the sleeves of her thin white sweater were pulled over her hands. "Do you know who lives here?"

She wiped at her eyes again, removing the last of the remaining tears. "Chris. He's got two roommates, but I don't remember their names."

Rand looked around. They were the only ones outside —all the trick-or-treaters had wrapped up.

"Let's pay Chris a visit."

And hope that nothing terrible happened here.

Stacy followed Rand up to the front door and he rang the doorbell. Music boomed from inside the house. The door opened and a college-aged guy in a blue-collared shirt appeared in the threshold. He gave Rand a weird look, but then he spotted Stacy. "Oh. Hey, Stacy. Happy Halloween."

"Hi, Chris."

"You okay?" He glanced at Rand.

"Yeah, I'm fine," Stacy said, turning her head away. Chris's eyes softened with concern.

"Rand Casey," Rand said, holding out his hand. Chris paused and then shook it.

"Hi. What can I do for you?"

"Did a couple of kids knock on your door earlier? Or ring your doorbell?"

"It's Halloween, man. Kids have been ringing my doorbell all night."

"I'm talking about two very specific kids. If they did, then you'd know what I mean."

Recognition dawned in Chris's eyes. "Maybe you ought to talk to Matt. He had some wild story about two creepy children that weren't wearing costumes. We all laughed at him."

"Is he here?" Rand asked.

"Yeah. Keep in mind that he's had about nine beers, even though he says he hasn't. Wait here."

Chris went to find his roommate.

"I can't believe this," Stacy whispered. "I'm not the only one this happened to."

Matt came to the door wearing nothing but a pair of shorts and flip flops and his skinny chest was pasty white. He carried a can of beer. He squinted at Rand as if he couldn't quite see him clearly.

"Are you Matt?" Rand asked.

"Who wants to know?"

"My name's Rand. I was talking to your buddy Chris just now. He said you answered the door when two strange kids rang your doorbell earlier this evening."

Matt's eyes went wide. "Man, those little fuckers freaked me out."

"What did they say to you?"

"They wanted to come in and use my telephone."

Stacy shot Rand a look. "And then?" he prodded.

"I thought they were lost, because they weren't wearing any costumes and I couldn't see their parents anywhere. They... they also didn't have any shoes. I don't know, it was just weird."

"You didn't let them in, did you?"

"Hell no. I told them to ask someone else because I lost my cell phone earlier today. Then they got mad at me. Started yelling at me. I had a bad feeling, so I slammed the door in their faces." Matt paused. "Wait, you're not, like, their dad or something, are you?"

"I'm not. The neighbors had a similar problem with these kids."

"Oh. Well, I hope they found their telephone. Who are they, anyway?"

"No one special. If they come back, don't let them in no matter what they say."

Matt scrunched his face. "Sure. If you say so, man."

"Have a good night. Try not to drink too much."

Matt took a long swig of his beer as he closed the door.

"That guy didn't fall for it," Stacy said. "Why did Kim have to?"

"If they knock on enough doors, then statistically speaking they're bound to find one person to let them in."

"Why did it have to be Kim?"

They returned to the street and once again picked up the trail of black footprints, which headed off the sidewalk and onto the road.

"Damn," Rand said.

"What?"

He swept the beam of light over the asphalt. "They've crossed here, but since their prints are black, it makes them hard to see."

Stacy stood beside him and helped him search. "Don't move the light so fast." She grabbed his hand with the flashlight and guided it slower along the street. She stopped it. "Right there. Is that it?"

Rand kept the light trained on the spot and leaned down. He could barely make out the black slime and the two footprints in them. "Yeah. Good work. Go slow and don't lose the trail."

The prints led them across the block and to the left. Rand stepped carefully, making sure to not accidentally smudge the tracks with his own shoe.

"These are getting thinner," Rand said.

"Look." Stacy grabbed his hand with the flashlight again and pointed it up. The bright beam illuminated one of the parked cars on the road—a white sedan. The plasma was streaked on the driver's side of the car. Children's black handprints were pressed onto the window. They contrasted with the car's white paint job.

Rand pointed his light toward the house that corresponded to where the vehicle was parked. "Looks like this person had a car visit."

"Do they approach people in cars, too?" Stacy asked.

"It's not unheard of," Rand said. "Come on."

Stacy followed Rand to the door and he rang the bell.

The person who came peeked out from behind the curtain and studied him for a long time.

The door cracked open and a college-aged girl looked at him through the sliver of space. "Do I know you?"

"My name is Rand Casey, and I wanted to ask you about your car."

The girl scrutinized him for a short while, then opened up the door a bit more. "What about my car?" She peered around her yard, surveying the area.

"Are you all right? You seem upset."

"It's just been a weird night," she said. "Sorry. I hate Halloween."

"I hate Halloween too. Again, I'm Rand, and this is Stacy."

"Veronica," said the girl.

Rand gestured over his shoulder. "I noticed your car is covered in something nasty."

Veronica folded her arms. "Yeah. I wanted to wash it

off, but I don't want to be out here tonight. I'll do it in the morning."

"Did something happen to you earlier?" Veronica looked away and tucked a loose strand of hair behind her ear. "I'm asking because we also had some weird things happen."

"Seems there's someone going around the neighborhood," Veronica said.

"Do you mind telling me what happened?" Rand kept his voice gentle. He could see the girl was on edge.

"I…" She searched for her words. "I came home from a friend's house and parked there. I looked down for a second because my purse was on the floor of the passenger seat. Then two little kids knocked on my window. It scared the crap out of me, because I hadn't seen them and then they were just there all of a sudden. I rolled down the window, and they wanted to get into my car because they needed a ride somewhere."

"Where did they want you to take them?"

"I don't know. They never said. I kept asking them where they needed to go, but then they yelled at me, telling me I was bad for not letting two innocent kids into my car, or something like that." Veronica shivered and looked as if she might cry. "I wanted to help them, because I figured they were lost. But then they freaked me out when they got angry. So I ran out of my car and into my house and locked the door."

"You did the right thing," Rand said. "These same boys have been knocking on other doors up and down the block, saying similar things. They're just Halloween pranksters."

"Well, whoever they are, they're really freaky. I still feel weird."

"They're gone now, but if they come back, don't let them in."

"If you say so," Veronica said.

"Thank you for your time. I hope the rest of your night goes better."

Veronica went back inside, as if she couldn't stand being exposed for another minute.

"What does it all mean?" Stacy asked Rand.

He didn't answer, and instead pondered Veronica's story as he returned to her white sedan. Once there, he shone his light around and scoped out the area, looking for the trail of footprints. "Do you see any more tracks?"

"No," Stacy said.

"It looks like they originated here. This was their first target."

"And it was a car instead of a house," Stacy added.

"Yeah."

It wasn't just about getting into the car, Rand thought. *They specifically asked to be taken somewhere...*

"What are you thinking?" Stacy asked.

Rand realized he'd been lost in thought for a long time. "I'm wondering about their request to be driven somewhere, rather than just wanting to get inside the car."

"What about it?"

"Do you think…"

"Yeah," Rand said, meeting Stacy's worried gaze. "I think the next step is finding out *where* these kids wanted to go. If it's a specific location, we might find Kim there because she didn't just vanish into thin air."

That was impossible. If she was alive, that meant they

took her. If the kids were looking for other victims to take, then that meant they had somewhere to keep them. Demonic entities were almost always tied to a place with a negative energy that attracted them and anchored them there.

Stacy looked like she was going to be sick. Rand anticipated her next question.

"And how do we find out?" she asked.

In every case Rand had been involved in, there always came a time to transition from an outside observer to a direct participant. At some point, if he was going to make progress, he had to get his hands dirty.

"I'll have to ask those two kids myself."

17

Rand and Stacy left Veronica's house and returned to where Rand had parked his Jeep in the middle of the road. It was about eleven o'clock. Lights in the windows of the surrounding houses had been turned off, leaving the neighborhood darker than it had been before.

"What will you do?" Stacy asked him.

Rand withdrew his car keys from his pocket. "I'll drive around the neighborhood until the kids come for me."

Stacy looked at him like he was crazy. "How do you know they will?"

"They're demonic entities, so chances are they know who I am. Demons show themselves to me when I *don't* want them, so I assume they'll be more than happy to oblige now that I do."

"Aren't you scared?"

"I'm trying not to think about that." Yes, the idea of seeking out the black-eyed kids chilled him inside. But he couldn't run away from his fear. "How far back does this neighborhood go?"

Stacy pointed down the block. "If you head this way, you can go either right or left. Both circle around on each other. It eventually opens up to the edge of campus on the other end."

"Got it."

"What about me? What should I do?"

"I think it's best if you come with me." He hated telling her that, but it was true.

"I knew you would say that." She closed her eyes and took a deep breath, as if psyching herself up. "I guess that's better than staying home alone."

"Exactly."

"But do we have to *look* for them?" Stacy asked. "Can't we just wait inside for them to knock?"

"We need to be in the car when they show up," Rand said. "From what we've heard tonight, if we're in the house, then they'll ask to come inside. But if we're driving, then they'll ask for a ride. Hopefully I can use that to find out where they want to go."

Miller said that the first reported account of a black-eyed kid sighting had happened to a person while he was in his car.

"I'm going to vomit," Stacy muttered.

"Let's get moving before we freak ourselves out too much."

"You mean you're not already scared enough?" Stacy went around to the passenger side of his Jeep.

Rand fired up the engine and began to cruise down the street, in no rush at all. As he drove, he kept his eyes peeled. The houses in the neighborhood were simple and clustered together, mostly rented by college kids. To Rand, it felt strange to seek out demonic entities in such an unassuming, ordinary place.

"Is this the kind of stuff you do for your cases?" Stacy asked.

"Yes. Although I've never done anything quite like this before."

Since Rand had never encountered black-eyed kids before, he was pretty much making things up as he went along. He didn't want to tell Stacy that, though.

Stacy peered out the window and shook her head. "I can't believe I'm part of one of your cases. How did that happen?"

Rand didn't respond. The question sounded rhetorical.

"How do you live like this?" Stacy asked him, her voice forlorn.

Rand had been asked that quite often. "I've been chosen. It's my job to help those who encounter the supernatural."

He came to an intersection and took a left turn. The compact houses continued on, and he drove carefully to avoid sideswiping any of the parked cars along the road.

"Chosen?" Stacy snorted. "Sounds more like you're cursed."

"That's what most people say. I've had to do a lot of soul searching to turn my perspective around. So now, I consider myself chosen."

"You always tell us we shouldn't mess with the occult," Stacy said. "You said if we do, then we attract these things into our lives. Maybe being in your class is enough. You fill my head with scary stories and images during your lessons, and then I go home and study the material. So now my whole life is math problems, balancing chemical equations, and demons."

Rand looked at her in the passenger seat. She still gazed out the window. "You should take a break. My tests are easy, and you're a straight-A student. You don't need to study to do well in my class."

"I have to study no matter what," Stacy said. "I've never had a B on any report card or transcript in my whole life. My older sister went all the way through medical school without getting a B in a single class, and my parents expect me to do the same. I'm not a gifted test taker like her, so I have to study my butt off to get the same results.

"I took your class because they said it was an easy A, but they also said the same thing about Biology 101 with Dr. Fraser. I focused on other classes, since Bio was supposed to be a given. But then the first test came and I realized I'd underestimated it too much. I made a C. I then realized that I'd have to give it *some* time. But the final grade was only averaged from three tests, so I over-prepared for the next two. I ended up with an A in the class, but it was the closest to a B I'd ever been. So when you say you're class is an easy A... I've been burned by that before."

"How about this," Rand said. "You don't have to take the midterm. I'll just give you an A. After everything you've been through tonight, you've earned it."

Stacy sighed. "What I should've done was take Ms. Sharma's class instead of yours. World Religions. I've heard her essays are killers, but at least there're no black-eyed kids."

Rand felt deflated. All the girl wanted to do was pass school and live up to her own steep expectations for herself. And here he was, the "chosen one," screwing it all up.

Something in his periphery caught his attention. He halted the Jeep at a four-way stop. There were no other cars at the intersection, so Rand idled there for a bit.

Stacy looked at him when she realized they weren't continuing on. "Why are you stopping? What do you see?"

Rand stared toward the side yard of the house on the corner. There was an oak tree there, and he could just make out a shadowy figure standing near it. Rand could recognize that shape anywhere.

Looks like Shindael is doing some trick-or-treating, he thought.

"Wait here," Rand said, throwing the Jeep in park. "Lock the doors."

"Where are you going?"

Rand left the Jeep idling at the four-way stop and crossed in front of the headlights, walking toward the tree where he'd spotted the demon. When he got there, Shindael wasn't there anymore, having disappeared the moment Rand took his eyes off him.

Typical, Rand thought.

He approached the oak tree and checked around the other side of the trunk. Nothing. The nearby streetlight was burned out, leaving the area in darkness. The only light came from inside the house. In the single window that looked out into the yard, Rand spotted a shadowy outline peering at him from behind the glass. Rand stared at the demon for a long time, the figure unmoving.

"Come out here and face me," Rand said out loud.

He turned his back on the window. Shindael had reappeared inches from him, just as Rand knew he would. The familiar feeling of dread and despair that he experienced whenever the demon was near bubbled up inside of him.

"Happy Halloween," Rand said.

Shindael remained still.

Rand understood Shindael to be different than the demons he usually encountered in his cases. Shindael ranked highly in hell, favored by the devil, and therefore commanded a legion of servants that did his bidding. He even had a unique appearance—common demons appeared as black shadows or as a combination of animals, while Shindael's skin was light blue, as if he were frozen. The back of his smooth head was elongated, which Rand thought resembled an alien's, and his eyes were small, slanted, and completely black.

Although Rand was never happy to see his nemesis, the sudden presence gave him an important clue.

"I assume you're behind all this. That the black-eyed kids are your servants." Shindael did not respond. "Where is the girl?" he demanded.

'God has abandoned you.' As always, Shindael communicated with Rand telepathically. The voice was a breathy whisper in his mind. *'You cannot bring yourself to read holy Scripture. You can no longer pray. That is because you know that God has forsaken you. He will not protect you from me.'*

Rand ground his teeth together and held Shindael's black gaze, even though the dark pools made him want to turn away.

Rand knew that Shindael could read his innermost thoughts, so he strived to keep his mind blank. He did not want to react, even if Shindael was right. The more separated Rand became from God, the more vulnerable he became. Shindael was well aware of that.

"I asked you a question," Rand said through clenched teeth. "Where is the girl?"

'I cannot give you what I do not have.'

"Why Kim? Why Stacy? What do either of them have to do with you? I'm the one you want, right? Why hurt them?"

'You are my plaything, Randolph. You have opposed my master, and for that you will pay. Your life is not enough. I have vowed to torment both you and those close to you as punishment for actions.'

Rand had heard as much before. Shindael had made that clear on the night they'd first encountered each other.

What frightened Rand about Shindael the most was the depth of the demon's power. It was clear he was in a position of authority in the hierarchy of hell, since all of the demons that Rand had faced lately were direct servants of Shindael. Such power meant that Shindael could reach out and kill Rand whenever he desired.

But with the demonic, it would never be that simple. Shindael desired more than mere death; he wanted chaos and destruction.

'I care nothing for the girl. Only you. She is nothing more than a piece of our game. When the sun rises, I will command my servants to deliver her into the hands of my master in hell.'

Rand swallowed. Kim was alive, but if Rand couldn't find her and rescue her before dawn…

It was exactly what Rand had come to expect from Shindael. He'd likely grown bored with killing humans thousands of years ago. Now he used them for his twisted amusement.

"Tell me where your servants are," Rand demanded.

'If you seek my servants, you will find them.'

"Yeah, that's what I'm doing. So if you can call them up and have them meet me, that'd be great. I don't have—"

Shindael's eyes flared red and his mouth gaped open, exposing sharp teeth. The demon's shadowy apparition lunged toward Rand, as if leaping to take a bite out of him. Rand flinched and covered his face with his arm, dropping onto the ground, bracing for the pain.

It never came.

"Mr. Casey."

Rand uncovered his eyes. Shindael had vanished and he was unharmed.

He's never come at me like that before, Rand thought. *Maybe he didn't appreciate the sass.*

"Mr. Casey!"

Rand looked toward Stacy's voice. She'd rolled down the car window and was shouting at him. Rand got up and returned to the Jeep, scanning the intersection for any sign of Shindael, but the demon had left him.

"Are you okay?" Stacy asked as he approached.

"Yes. I'm fine."

"Who were you talking to?" Stacy asked.

"An old friend."

"But… there's nobody there."

Rand wiped at his face. It was slick was sweat.

"Were you seeing someone? Or something?" Stacy gave him a sympathetic yet questioning look.

Rand exhaled. Given what Stacy had been through so far that night, it seemed fair to let her know what they dealing with.

"Shindael." Even uttering the name took his breath away.

"What?"

"A demon that follows me. He punishes me for all the times I've defeated his servants."

Stacy's eyes fell to her lap as she pursed her lips. "This demon has something to do with what's going on tonight?"

"Yes."

"He's making the black-eyed kids do this?"

Rand nodded.

"Does he know where Kim is?"

Rand had to be careful with his words. He wanted Stacy to be informed, but to still remain as calm as she could manage. "We have to find her before dawn."

Stacy kept her eyes down. She sniffled and cleared her throat. "Or else what?"

"There's plenty of time." Rand forced his tone to sound confident and sure. "We'll get to her. I promise."

Stacy wiped at her eyes and glanced at the digital clock on the dashboard.

It was just after midnight.

"But—" Something caught her eye further down the street. "Oh my God." She pointed.

Two child-sized shadows stood side-by-side about twenty yards down the road. The streetlight ahead spilled a yellow glow onto them, but they still only looked like black figures, as if they were immune to the illumination.

"That's them," Rand said.

Rand rushed around the front of the Jeep and got behind the wheel.

"Don't do it, Mr. Casey," Stacy begged, unable to take her eyes off the two kids. "There has to be another way."

"They won't hurt you as long as I'm with you." It

wasn't necessarily true, but he hoped that would reassure her.

He inched the Jeep forward toward the pair. They stood in the middle of the street, making no effort to get out of his way. When he'd closed the distance, his headlights flickered, blinked, and then went out.

"What did you do that for?" Stacy asked, voice tense.

"I didn't."

The streetlight extinguished.

Demons didn't like the light. They shut them off whenever possible.

Rand gripped the steering wheel, wondering if he should make the first move. Beside him, Stacy breathed in sharp, terrified gasps.

The two walked around the side of the Jeep toward the driver's-side window. The taller of the pair lifted his hand and knocked three times.

Although every instinct in Rand's body implored him not to, he rolled down the window.

"We need you to give us a ride."

It was the taller one who spoke. His voice was high-pitched like a child's, but he sounded very... off. His words were very clear, precise, and direct, unlike a normal kid.

"Get in," Rand said.

18

Boyd Street was chaos.

Hundreds of costumed college students crammed onto the narrow road. Music blared from the nearby houses, from the parked cars, and from speakers set up on the front lawns. Although the night was chilly, the dense crowds generated heat, causing Libby to sweat underneath her heavy costume.

Libby and her friends arrived at the party in silence and confusion. The incident with the kids had killed their mood.

Libby surveyed the area. There was so much going on, but none of it distracted her from the horrible feeling she had. The hunting bow slung over her shoulder seemed heavy now, and although her boots were comfortable, her feet ached; she'd been standing for hours and her sudden spike of fear had left her emotionally drained and fatigued.

She felt a hand on her arm. "You okay?" Bailey asked, concerned.

"I don't think so," she said, keeping her voice low so that Parker wouldn't hear. "That was just…"

"I know. Come on. We can forget about it now."

Terrance was also subdued. He had not liked how they had blown off the kids. Libby admired him for his concern, but she knew it was misplaced.

Parker, who led the group into the Boyd Street crowds, turned and clapped his hands to command their attention. "Enough of this downer stuff. We're here for a good time, and we're going to have it. My buddies are around somewhere, so we'll hook up with them and get tonight started right. Come on."

He pushed through the crowds, his broad antlers coming close to striking other partiers.

Libby and Bailey followed, arms linked, with Terrance a few steps behind. Libby appreciated that Parker was attempting to fix the mood, but she knew she was too far gone to get a second wind.

They passed by a group of people surrounding a beer keg. Three guys lifted the legs of a large, costumed man, trying to position him to do a keg stand, but they weren't strong enough to support his weight. Two others orbited around them, filming on their cell phones while laughing.

"Come on, lift him up." one of them shouted.

The rest in the crowd chanted. "Mill-er. Mill-er. Mill-er."

Libby paused. She stared at the upside-down man, wondering if she was seeing things. His costume kept her from seeing if it was really him.

"Libby?" Bailey said. Parker had not realized she'd stopped and had trudged onward.

"You go ahead," Libby told her. "I'll catch up with you in a minute."

Bailey and Terrance followed Parker and disappeared into the crowd.

Libby approached the keg-stand fiasco. The three bros finally got the legs high enough and the big man put the spout into his mouth and drank while the crowds whooped in encouragement. One of the supporting guys lost his strength and dropped out. The sudden shift in weight caused the other two to lose control and their friend fell, landing hard on his side and then rolling onto his back. Beer sprayed from his lips in a foamy mess. Everyone cheered and laughed, and the guy filming on his cell phone zoomed in on the fallen man.

After a few moments, a couple guys helped him up. He was dressed like a portable toilet, and it was definitely him.

They met eyes at the same time. Libby saw the confusion that crossed Miller Landingham's face.

Libby walked over to him. "Miller? What are you doing here?"

"Umm…" Miller looked around, wiping beer from his chin. "Maybe I could ask you the same thing."

Libby folded her arms. "Are you going to tell on me?"

"Not if you don't tell on me."

Libby stuck out her hand and they shook.

"We were at the school's Halloween dance, but then we came here," Libby said. "I don't feel like being here, though. I'd rather go home."

"Does your dad know you're here?"

"Of course not. You?"

"Hell no. He stopped by the shop earlier and made sure I wasn't going to leave. I lied to him."

"Same, but at my mom's house. Mom and Bill are going to Bill's company's party, so everyone is sneaking around behind Dad's back."

Miller shrugged. His entire costume shifted up when he did. "We have to. Otherwise no one gets to have any Halloween fun. What's Rando up to tonight, anyway?"

"He said was staying in, same as every year."

She imagined her dad at home, peeking through the windows like a paranoid person. He was likely proud of himself for forcing his family and friends to stay inside like him, when in reality none of them were obeying.

She remembered the two boys she had seen and hated to admit that maybe, this time, her dad had been right.

Libby eyed Miller's group. There were about seven college guys, and they were upending another of their friends over the beer keg. This guy went more easily than Miller had.

"How do you know these dudes?"

"Long story."

"Come on."

"Uh… well, the bookstore is strapped for cash. I do a couple things on the side to make extra money. I buy them alcohol from time to time, and charge them a fee."

Libby only shook her head. "Seriously?"

"I gotta do what I gotta do."

"But… that doesn't explain why you're here."

"They invited me. How else were they going to get a keg? And besides, what else was I going to do tonight? Oh, and your dad has no idea about this little side hustle, so that stays between you and me, all right?"

"Sure."

Miller eyed her. "You okay?"

"Yeah…" She debated telling him about the creepy kids. He'd believe her; they'd both had plenty of run-ins with evil. But a single isolated encounter was not always something to worry about. It came with the territory when you associated with Randolph Casey. Besides, she didn't want to put a damper on Miller's Halloween. He had worked just as hard to maneuver around her dad.

"I'm fine. Just tired."

"Head home, then. This place is crazy and gets more intense every year."

"I'll try. But I'm with a group."

"If you want me to find you a way home, let me know."

"Thanks, Miller. And nice costume."

He patted his chest. "Couldn't pass it up."

Libby left him and pushed through the crowds, searching for her friends. As she got closer to the middle of Boyd Street, she realized the party was far more crowded than she'd thought. All around her she saw witches, zombies, and more than a handful of partygoers dressed up like the president. She brushed past a girl in a sexy devil costume, who had spilled beer on her camo shirt. A soldier and a cowboy erupted into a fist fight. The surrounding people reacted instantly and swarmed to form a circle around them, shouting and cheering. Libby got caught up in their motion, her entire body shifted by the sudden force of the crowds. She fought to regain control and pushed against the masses, getting as far from the brawl as she could.

When she burst through, a wave of light-headedness

passed through her. Cold sweat broke out on her forehead, and she closed her eyes.

I don't feel well. It had come on suddenly. Maybe she was feeling claustrophobic. Or perhaps she was just more tired than she thought and all the people were causing too much chaos.

I'll never find my friends like this. I need to call them and set a place to meet—

She felt a small hand slide into her palm and clasped her fingers. Like that of a child.

Libby opened her eyes. When she looked down, she saw him—the younger of the two kids they had encountered on the way to Boyd Street. Only his mop of long, tangled hair was visible. He did not look up at her, only straight ahead.

Sudden pain pounded in her temples. The sounds of the party around her lessened, as if she'd put in earplugs. Libby was frozen in place. She wanted to pull away from the kid, but couldn't for some reason. She should've been much stronger than him.

The boy started walking. He pulled Libby along by the hand and she had to follow. That, or be dragged. He had surprising strength, and when she finally found the will inside her to resist, he only clutched her fingers tighter, sending crushing pain into her bones.

Libby was led through the crowds. The edges of her vision blurred, and she felt like she was about to faint. The crowds parted for the kid. People did not seem to see either Libby or the boy.

Where are you taking me?

Somehow, she knew the boy could read her thoughts.

But there was no answer. Then another frightening thought occurred to her.

Where is the other one?

Although she struggled to see clearly, some people they passed struck her as odd. They wore costumes that looked like throwbacks—maybe to the 1980s.

They stopped walking, and Libby immediately saw the other boy straight ahead of her. He stood ten paces away with his hands by his side. His black eyes bored into Libby, and an icy chill spread through her entire body. She knew without a doubt that these two kids were evil, and that she had to flee from them. The smaller one still clasped her hand.

There was a girl standing beside the other black-eyed kid. She wore a cheerleader Halloween costume and held a beer. She leaned against a guy, whose arm was around her while he talked to one of his friends and paid her no mind. The girl looked down at the kid, eyes wide and filled with fear.

She can see him, too, Libby realized.

The girl, without taking her gaze from the boy beside her, used her free hand to slap her boyfriend's side, trying to get his attention. He ignored her.

Run, Libby tried to shout, but she couldn't hear her own voice. All sounds around her had somehow drained away.

The cheerleader couldn't hear Libby either.

The older boy smiled at Libby.

'Do you want to see me hurt her?' The voice filled Libby's head, loud and dark like an otherworldly growl.

In her desperation, Libby remembered what she

needed to do—what her dad had always taught her to do. *In the name of Jesus Christ, I command you to leave.*

If they truly were evil, they were compelled to obey if commanded in the name of the Lord. But Libby's voice was muted once again.

The boy opened his mouth wide, revealing sharp and jagged teeth. Black smoke spilled from his throat. He turned and clamped down hard on the cheerleader's leg just beneath the hem of her skirt. She screamed, dropped her beer, and collapsed to the ground. Everyone around her was startled by her sudden outburst.

Libby wanted to cry out, and she quickly looked to her side. The younger kid who held Libby's hand snarled up at her now, his black eyes narrowed in anger.

In the name—

The kid swiped at Libby with his free hand, moving at blinding speed. Pain erupted in her arm, as if she'd been sliced with a knife, and she shrieked. A moment later, the boy was gone.

Libby fell to her knees, clasping her left elbow where it hurt. The other evil boy had also vanished.

Everyone surrounded the cheerleader, who had collapsed and was holding her bitten thigh.

Libby looked down at her own arm. Three long gashes were ripped into the sleeve of her camo shirt and blood seeped from the burning wounds.

She stood and rushed over to the crying cheerleader.

"What the hell did you do to yourself?" demanded the guy she'd been leaning on.

Libby dropped to where the injured girl sat on the pavement. "Are you okay?"

"He bit me," the girl said through her tears.

"I saw him too."

Terror filled her eyes. "Really?"

"Yes." Libby held out her bloodied, scratched arm. "He did this to me."

"Who was he? Why did he do this?"

The girl's boyfriend hoisted her up, forcing her to stand. Libby also stood. "She needs to go home."

"Yeah, no shit," he said, annoyed. "She's drunk and somehow cut herself." He rolled his eyes. "She's always ruining the night because she can't hold her liquor." The guy pulled her away.

"What was that thing?" the girl called to Libby as she was dragged, but soon the couple disappeared into the crowd.

The pain in Libby's head was gone, as was her blurry vision. The sound of the party returned in full force, and the only sign that the evil kids had ever been there were the bloody scratches on her left arm.

Libby knew that something was terribly wrong. These creatures were not only going to appear once as an isolated incident.

Miller.

She rushed back the way she'd come, pushing past drunken guys and girls, not caring about shoving them.

"Libby."

She saw Bailey standing with Terrance and Parker. Parker was talking to one of his friends, the same one from the dance earlier. Libby kept running. She had to find Miller.

When she got back to the place with the beer keg, the big portable toilet was nowhere to be found. Libby recognized the guy who'd been filming with his cell phone, and she grabbed him with both hands.

"Where's Miller?"

"Whoa. Chill, girl."

"Where is he?"

"He's right there. Let go of me."

Libby followed his pointing finger and spotted Miller near a parked truck. He and two other guys had lined up a bunch of shots on the lowered tailgate.

Libby rushed over, and just before Miller got the small glass to his mouth, she swatted it out of his hands. It shattered on the asphalt. She threw her arms around him and hugged him tightly, relieved to be in the presence of a friendly face.

"Libby? Are you okay? What happened?"

"There's something here, Miller," she said between sobs. "I don't know what it is, but it's evil."

Miller pulled her away from his friends. "What do you mean? Oh, you're bleeding?"

"He scratched me," Libby showed him her arm. She rolled up her ripped sleeve to reveal three red, glistening wounds.

Miller held her wrist and inspected them. Fear crossed his face. "This happened just now?"

"Yes. There are two of them. One did this to me, and the other made me watch while he bit someone else."

Miller pursed his lips and looked away. Libby knew what he was about to say, because she was thinking the same thing.

"We have to call your dad."

19

"**G**et in," Rand said.

The two boys opened the Jeep's back door and slid into the seat behind Rand and Stacy. The door closed by itself, as if with magic.

Rand idled for a minute, waiting for the kid to speak again. An uneasy tension bloomed. Stacy was stiff in the passenger seat, eyes fixed ahead.

"Where are we going?" Rand asked.

"We need you to take us home."

Rand waited for more information. He used his mirror to peer into the backseat, but the pair was covered in a darkness that did not seem natural.

"We're just two little kids!" the boy shouted at Rand, as if frustrated they weren't moving. Both Rand and Stacy jolted at the outburst. "We aren't going to hurt you."

To Rand, it sounded like the boy was reading off a cue card with no other context.

"Right," Rand said. "We'll take you home."

Rand shifted into drive and coasted down the road. As

he did, he noticed that Stacy had started trembling and seemed to be trying her best to hold it together.

Rand drove down a street that led him out of the neighborhood and onto a boulevard. He idled at the stop sign and allowed two cars to pass before he turned left.

"Where is home?" Rand asked. "Where exactly am I taking you?"

Rand tightened his grip on the steering wheel. He could feel the two kids in the backseat; their presence was powerful and heavy, as if some invisible force was pulling his entire body toward the ground underneath his Jeep. Rand had experienced that feeling many times in the past. Evil spirits often had an aura of negativity surrounding them that grew more distinct the closer they were.

"Where are we going?" Rand asked again.

I can honestly say I never thought I'd give a demon a lift, he thought.

As they drove, Rand tried his best to keep his attention on the two shadows in the rear. Although he ran over bumps and uneven patches in the road, causing him and Stacy to sway with the moving of the vehicle, the kids remained completely still as if the forces of physics did not apply to them.

He passed Gavin's Deli on his left. Rand was so surprised that his focus on the black-eyed kids faltered. He looked over his shoulder as the fast-food joint faded in the distance.

"What?" Stacy whispered, alarmed.

"Nothing," Rand said. He thought Gavin's Deli had gone out of business and no longer existed. *Miller used to love that place*.

Something else caught Rand's eye in the rearview

mirror. It was a car far behind him on the boulevard, speeding up and gaining on him fast.

The black sedan flashed its lights, signaling for Rand to move out of the way. There was an empty lane on either side of him, though, so Rand stayed put. The car tailgated Rand, lights flashing on and off and horn blaring.

"What's going on?" Stacy asked. "Mr. Casey, he's crazy, just get out of his way."

Rand realized what was happening and held his ground. It had been a long time since he'd encountered a phantom vehicle. It was a common demonic trick. The black-eyed kids were using it to attack him.

"Mr. Casey," Stacy said.

"This won't work on me," Rand said, glaring into the rearview mirror.

Finally, the black car swerved around him and sped past. It drifted recklessly across all the boulevard lanes, then disappeared into the distance ahead. As it went, Rand looked for a license plate. Just as he'd predicted, there was none.

"What in the world?" Stacy said. She gripped the center console and the passenger door's armrest.

"It wasn't real," Rand told her.

Stacy gasped. "You mean that was one of those ghost cars you teach us about?"

"Yes." Rand checked the two kids in the backseat again. They were still there, unmoving. "We can thank our little friends for that."

"Oh my God," she whispered.

Rand had occasionally seen phantom cars when he was involved in a case. They appeared to drive insanely and did whatever they could to get him to crash. The key to handling them was to recognize what they were as soon as possible, understand that they weren't real, and hold your ground.

There had been a handful of other cars on the boulevard when Rand had first turned onto it, but now it was empty. *Too* empty. It was late at night, sure, but this main thoroughfare usually had at least a few motorists during the night.

Two bright lights flashed in the distance ahead.

"Mr. Casey." Stacy reached over and grabbed Rand's arm.

The headlights grew brighter as the car sped toward them, going the wrong way in their lane.

"It's back," Rand told her. "Close your eyes, Stacy."

"What are you doing?"

Rand heard the sounds of the oncoming car's revving engine as it zoomed toward his Jeep. Rand grasped his steering wheel with both hands, knuckles white, and maintained his course.

"It's going to ram us!" Stacy shouted.

"No it won't. Stacy, close your eyes."

Rand leaned forward, ready for what appeared to be a head-on collision.

It'll go right through us, he thought. *They always do. It isn't real.*

The phantom vehicle wanted him to swerve. To dodge. To flip his car or crash. But Rand would not fall for its trick.

The black sedan made no signs of diverting.

At the last moment, Stacy screamed and lunged, grabbing the steering wheel and yanking it to the right. The

Jeep jerked into the other lane just as the phantom vehicle sped past, narrowly missing them. Rubber squealed on the road as Rand tried to regain control of the skidding Jeep. He turned into the swerve, trying not to panic, and then he straightened out.

An icy chill passed through Rand's entire body, the sickening nerves sprouting from a disaster just nearly avoided.

"What are you doing?" Rand shouted. "I told you to close your eyes."

"I'm sorry. I couldn't—" Tears leaked from Stacy's eyes.

Rand caught himself and contained his anger. Stacy had never been in such a situation before. She had reacted instinctively, and he couldn't blame her.

"How can you be sure that it wasn't real? It looked like it was. I'm *so* sorry, Mr. Casey, but—"

Rand gripped her forearm. "It's okay. We're fine. It doesn't matter now."

Stacy's wiped her eyes and sniffled, exhaling slowly.

"Everything's all right now," Rand said.

Red and blue lights flashed behind him, followed by the single blare of a police car's siren.

20

R and swore.

Stacy looked into her side mirror. The bright lights lit up her face. "Is it another ghost car?"

"I don't think so."

Of course the cops are out tonight, Rand thought. *And here I am, swerving all over the place.*

Rand honestly would have preferred to deal with another phantom vehicle. At least he could predict those. Rand had had very bad experiences when the police got involved in his supernatural cases.

"Mr. Casey?" Stacy prodded.

Rand put on his blinker and drifted to the shoulder. He would comply and work his best charm to convince the officer that nothing was wrong. Hopefully before the black-eyed kids caused any issues.

The police cruiser followed Rand and came to a stop several feet behind the Jeep. The two shadows remained silent and still. The bright lights from the police car did not seem to reach them. Rand waited for what felt like an eternity for the officer to make his move.

"What do we do?" Stacy whispered.

"Just be cool. I'll handle it."

The police officer approached, and Rand rolled down the window. "Evening, officer."

"License and registration." The officer shone his flashlight inside the Jeep. He was a young man with a slight build and a gentle face, even though he tried to exude authority.

Rand reached to his glove box and withdrew the registration papers, then pulled his driver's license from his wallet and handed them over.

The officer inspected them with his flashlight. "Do you know why I pulled you over, Mr. Casey?"

"I'm guessing because of that little swerve. I had one hell of a sneeze."

The officer shone the light back on Rand and eyed him. "Have you had anything to drink tonight, Mr. Casey?"

"Nothing."

He aimed the light at Stacy, inspected her for a moment, and then checked the rear of the vehicle. The officer's stony expression melted away and was replaced by uncertainty. Rand assumed the officer was starting to feel the dark aura that emanated from the black-eyed kids.

The flashlight blinked out.

Shit, Rand thought.

The officer slapped and shook it, jiggling the batteries. He clicked the button on and off, but it did not light up. He took a step back from the Jeep, and his hand went to the gun on his belt. Rand knew the other man's gut was telling him that something was off.

"Get out of the car, Mr. Casey."

Rand lifted his palms. "Is there a problem, officer?"

"I said get out of the car." A stern command this time.

Rand had no choice. He opened the car and slowly climbed out of the Jeep.

"Keep those hands where I can see them." The officer gripped Rand's arm and guided him toward the front of the car. "Hands on the hood."

Rand complied. The officer began to pat Rand down, first his jacket, then his jeans, then ankles.

"Carrying anything I need to know about?" the officer asked.

"No, sir."

"Who's the girl?"

"My girlfriend." Rand hated to lie, but the truth—that she was his student—sounded worse.

The officer's hands paused when he said that. "She looks young. Am I going to find something I don't like if I check her ID?"

"No, sir. Check it if you want."

The officer hesitated, as if considering whether to verify that or move on. He walked toward the back of the Jeep and spoke into the radio that was clipped onto on his shirt at the shoulder. "Barry, can you run a plate for me?"

"Go ahead, Joe."

Officer Joe read off Rand's license plate number.

"Got it," Barry said.

Joe returned to Rand. Rand saw the shadowed heads of the black-eyed kids turning in unison as they tracked Joe's movement. Watching him.

"Who are the kids?" Joe asked.

"Stacy's brothers." He nodded his head toward the passenger seat. "We took them trick-or-treating."

"Bit late for that, don't you think?"

The radio burst with static. "Hey Joe."

The officer reached to his shoulder and pushed the button. "What you got for me?"

The radio garbled. Barry's voice cut in and out.

Joe pressed the button again. "Repeat."

Rand glanced at the black-eyed kids again. They still watched Joe.

Oh, no.

He knew well how demons interfered with electronic equipment. Especially radios.

"The Jeep is registered to Randolph Casey," Barry said. His voice sounded different this time. Flat and distant. "Louisiana resident, address eight-one-three Plaster Road."

Rand's ears perked up. That wasn't his address.

"Anything on record?" Joe asked.

"He's been busy," Barry said. "Lots on his file. Murder, rape, incest, fornication with animals."

Joe froze, then furrowed his brow. "What was that?"

Barry's voice grew louder. "That's right, Joe. Randolph Casey likes to *fuck* animals."

Barry started to laugh. An inhuman, mirthless laugh.

"That isn't—" Rand began.

"Barry, what—"

"You need to shoot him, Joe. You need to shoot him *right now*." Barry cackled again.

Rand could tell Joe was both frightened and confused

and didn't know what to do. So he drew his gun and pointed it Rand. "Get on the ground."

"Whoa." Rand's body wanted to dodge out of the way of the gun barrel, but he forced himself to remain still. Stacy shrieked inside the car.

"On the ground!"

"Okay, okay." Rand flattened himself on the pavement. "Listen to me, Joe. That isn't your colleague on the radio."

"You're messing with my radio somehow," Joe said, although he sounded unconvinced. Like he was merely trying to make sense of what was happening.

"I didn't do anything," Rand said.

"I'm taking you in," Joe said.

"Don't arrest him," the radio blared. It wasn't Barry's voice at all anymore. It was inhuman. "Kill him. Shoot him, Joe. Kill him. Kill him *now*."

Joe ripped the radio from his shirt and threw it to the pavement as if the voice grated unbearably on his ears. "What the hell is this?"

A deep, otherworldly roar bellowed from inside Rand's Jeep. Both he and Joe snapped their heads toward it, caught off guard. The entire car lurched, rocking side to side as if two monsters were fighting inside.

"Stacy," Rand called out, and almost pushed himself up off the asphalt.

"Don't move," Joe shouted, bringing his gun closer to Rand's back.

Another growl, louder than the first. Stacy shrieked inside the car.

Joe's wide eyes darted back and forth between the Jeep and Rand.

"What are you waiting for?" Rand shouted at Joe. "Get her out of there."

"Stay right where you are." Joe lowered his gun and rushed to the passenger side of the Jeep. Rand heard him throw open the door.

"Ma'am, are you—"

"Let me out of here!" Stacy screamed.

From where Rand lay, he saw Stacy's feet land on the street and run around the front of the Jeep. She was kneeling over him and clawing desperately at his clothes, trying to get him to stand up.

"Where are those kids?" Joe asked.

Stacy forced Rand to his feet with surprising strength. He wanted to stay on the ground to avoid more trouble, but Stacy was no longer acting rationally. Her face was flushed red and her blonde hair was disheveled. The black-eyed kids had done something to her.

"Hey," Joe barked. Rand and Stacy froze, standing together, eyes on Joe. "Where the hell are the kids? Where did they go?"

Rand had no idea. But whatever the kids had done, they had scared Stacy almost to death. *Maybe even hurt her.*

"They…" Stacy began, her voice trembling.

A black shadow began to leak from the open doors of Rand's Jeep and float up toward the sky like smoke. The tendrils blended with the darkness of the night and seemed to vanish toward the sky.

They're leaving, Rand thought. He'd seen many demons leave behind a shadowy, smoke-like substance when they disappeared.

Joe watched the shadow as it drifted toward the sky,

transfixed. His mouth moved as if trying to say something, but no words came out.

When the shadow had vanished from sight, Joe cast Rand and Stacy a frightened, helpless look. He now seemed deeply disturbed.

Joe turned and fled. He leapt back into his police cruiser and sped away.

"Are you okay?" Rand asked Stacy. "What the hell happened?"

Stacy lifted a trembling hand and gripped the collar of her t-shirt. She pulled it down, revealing a dark red handprint seared into the skin on her shoulder. A fresh wave of sobs came when she saw it.

"Fuck. One of them touched you," Rand said.

Rand had suffered many marks just like it. They tended to burn pretty badly at first, but the pain usually subsided after a few hours.

Stacy swallowed and fought to calm down so she could speak. "I'm sorry, but I didn't know what else to do. Those kids were making all that stuff happen with the police officer, so I started praying and commanding them to leave in the name of Jesus like you taught us in class and they got mad and started growling and rocking the car and one of them grabbed me and—"

"Shh… shh… it's okay," Rand said. "You were absolutely right that they were causing this, and you did the right thing."

Stacy sniffed and tried to suppress her tears. She still held her shirt away from the handprint, appearing nervous the cotton would irritate it.

A horn blew and a car swerved around Rand's parked Jeep. Then another.

After a long time of the boulevard being devoid of any other cars, the other motorists had finally reappeared, seemingly all at once.

"Where did all these cars come from?" Rand asked as he guided Stacy toward the passenger seat. He wondered if the black-eyed kids had also somehow caused the boulevard to clear with some kind of supernatural ability. Likely, but he didn't have time to think about it just then. "Come on. Let's get off the road." He helped Stacy in and closed her door.

As he walked around to the driver's side, another car maneuvered around his Jeep. This one slowed and the man behind the wheel gave Rand a look of concern through his rolled-down window. "You all right?"

"All good, thanks," Rand said, giving a polite wave.

The man seemed unconvinced, but Rand hopped back into his Jeep, fired up the engine, and pulled off into the nearby parking lot of a hotel.

Rand rested on the back of his car seat. Fire still pumped though his body. His heart seemed to bang in his ears. Nervous sweat dampened his flesh.

When he turned toward Stacy, he caught her examining the red handprint on her shoulder again.

"I've had dozens of those. It'll fade."

"I can't believe it," she said, not taking her eyes away. "It's just like those pictures you show us in class."

Rand wished he could take that mark from her. If it weren't for him, that never would have happened.

"I screwed up the plan," Stacy said.

Rand twisted in his seat to face her more fully. "What do you mean? You *saved* me back there. I was about to be arrested."

Stacy let the collar of her shirt fall back over the hand-print as if she could no longer bear to look at it. "We had a plan. Find the black-eyed kids make them take us to Kim. But when I saw how they were tricking that police officer and how much trouble you were in, the only thing I could think to do was chase them away with the commands you taught us in class. And now they're gone and we don't know where Kim is." She shook her head and fumbled with a frayed strand of denim on her jeans, as if ashamed to make eye contact.

"Eight-one-three Plaster Road," Rand said, surprising himself by how the memory seemed to spill from his mouth.

Stacy looked at him. "Huh?"

"Eight-one-three Plaster Road," Rand repeated. "When the black-eyed kids were projecting their voices over the officer's radio, that was the address they gave for me. But that isn't my address."

Rand slid his phone from his pocket and typed the address into the GPS app. The map zoomed onto a location at the edge of the city.

"It's a real address," Rand said.

From what Rand could tell, Plaster Road was a long, rural highway with many curves and bends through a heavily wooded area.

"I've never heard of it." Stacy shifted to get a better look at Rand's phone.

He held it out so she could see. "Me either. But look, it's way out there on the northern part of town. I think it actually might be outside the city limits."

"Why here?" Stacy asked. Her and Rand's faces were inches apart as they studied the map.

Rand could only come up with one explanation. "Demons are master liars, as you've learned in class, but that doesn't necessarily mean they just pull stuff out of their asses. The things they say are either things that they know, or are meaningful to them in some way." Rand used his thumbs to zoom in on the area, but there wasn't much detail on the map. "If they spouted off this address, that means this location is important to them for some reason."

"Do you think that's where they're keeping Kim?" A hopeful note had slipped into Stacy's tone.

"I can't say for sure," Rand said. "But this is the best clue I have."

Rand's phone started ringing in his hand, displacing the GPS app.

Libby.

His heart dropped. It was after midnight and there *should* be no reason for her to call at that hour.

"Libby," he said, bringing the phone to his ear, voice cracking.

"Dad." Her voice sounded like she'd been crying. "Something's happened."

21

R and waited in that hotel parking lot for what felt like ages. Libby had wanted to explain what had happened over the phone, but once Rand realized she was out of the house and with Miller, he told her to come to him.

He paced back and forth near his Jeep, Stacy watching him worriedly. She'd stopped asking him questions once she'd realized how upset he was.

Rand wondered if they did this every year. Told him that they were going to stay in and behave just to placate him, only to go out and party on the most dangerous night of the year.

He felt angry and betrayed, but he had to file that away for later. For now, he needed to make sure his daughter was okay.

Miller's old pickup truck turned into the hotel parking lot. Before it came to a complete stop, Libby bolted from the passenger seat and ran over to Rand, throwing her arms around his neck and pulling him into a tight squeeze.

"Are you okay?" Rand asked.

"I don't know," she said, the tears starting again.

"Tell me what happened."

Miller killed the engine and joined them. Rand gave his friend's portable toilet Halloween costume a single irritated glance before turning his attention back to his daughter.

He saw her arm. Three scratches had torn through her camo shirt, leaving red lines in her pale skin. "You were attacked."

"I'm sorry," she said, wiping her tears away. "It's just—"

"Just tell me what happened. And the truth this time, please."

Libby exhaled. "I wanted to go to the Halloween dance at school. You know, do something normal on Halloween for once. I knew you'd never let me, so I didn't tell you. Bailey and Mom were in on it too.

"Anyway, I predicted you'd come check everything out, so we set up a fake study party at Mom's house. As soon as you were gone, Bailey and I got into our costumes and went to the dance.

"The guy who took me to the dance wanted to go to Boyd Street, so we went. On the way to the party, we ran into these two creepy kids. I got a really bad feeling from them. Like, I knew there was just something totally *wrong* about them and that they didn't belong. We ended up running away.

"We got to the party and I saw Miller there." Miller hung his head like a kid getting ratted out for misbehavior. "I hoped that nothing else was going to happen, but then the kids appeared again. One of them grabbed my hand and I couldn't get away. It was like I was frozen. I did what you've always told me to do—I commanded them to leave in the name of God, and that's when the one holding my hand scratched me and vanished. The other one bit a girl on the leg. Then I ran and found Miller, and now we're here."

Rand rubbed at his temples with his fingers, pressing into them. A headache had started to form behind his eyes, and not because of his proximity to demonic entities. This one was from fatigue and mental exhaustion from all the adrenaline rushes he'd had that night.

"What have you been doing, Rando?" Miller asked. "You look like hell."

"Why haven't you taken off that costume?" Rand said. "You look ridiculous."

Miller shed the portable toilet, leaving him in nothing but faded blue jeans and a white t-shirt covered in sweat. As he did, Rand shared his side of the events.

"So this has escalated beyond ringing doorbells." Miller said.

"We have a legitimate emergency," Rand said.

"And you said you have an address?"

Rand held up his phone, GPS flashing the location. "Stacy and I were just about to head out there, but then y'all called."

Miller ran a hand through his sweaty hair. "I can't believe you invited them into your car. You specifically did what I told you *not* to do."

"So did both of you," Rand said, glaring.

"Lecture us later," Miller shot back. "What's the address you managed to get?"

"Eight-one-three Plaster Road," Rand said.

Miller whistled. "Plaster Road, huh. That's a blast from the past."

"You know it?"

"You don't? It's one of the oldest areas in town. They fought hard decades ago to not be included in the city limits. Those properties have been there for generations."

Old homes, Rand thought. *This is starting to make more sense.* Old homes were far more likely to attract negative spirits.

"What should Libby and I do?" Miller asked.

"You both are coming with me," Rand said. Miller and Libby exchanged a glance. "That's right. Being alone and separated seems to provoke more encounters. If we stay as a group, we decrease those chances."

Rand would have preferred to send them home and keep them as far away from this mess as possible. But after hearing about Libby's encounter, Rand realized that the black-eyed kids could appear anywhere. The best place for Miller and Libby, at least at the moment, was where he could keep an eye on them.

Rand got behind the wheel of his Jeep while Miller climbed into the passenger seat. Libby and Stacy crawled into the back, occupying the spaces where the black-eyed kids had been just twenty minutes before.

When Rand fired up the ignition, the digital clock on the center console lit up. It read 12:43.

He tapped the clock with his index finger, drawing Miller's attention to it.

"The blue bastard showed up," Rand said, keeping his voice low. "We have until dawn."

Miller's expression became grim.

As Rand pulled out of the parking lot, he hoped he would find something useful on Plaster Road. Something that would give him a clue as to what to do next. Hopefully it would lead him to Kim.

Deep down, he knew it would not be that simple.

22

As Rand drove, a heavy silence fell over them all, one punctuated by anxiety, exhaustion, and fear.

It was only broken when Libby said to Stacy. "I'm Libby. His daughter."

"I'm Stacy. I take his class."

Rand followed the blue highlighted road on his phone's GPS outside of the city limits, and soon enough he came to an intersection. An old street sign, small and barely legible in the night, indicated that it was Plaster Road. He turned right.

Miller was correct—Rand could tell it was one of the oldest roads in the region. It was narrow, curved, and not well maintained. There were no streetlights, so Rand had to switch on his brights and take the turns very slowly. Trees lined the road on either side; it had been paved through the woods. They created the illusion of driving through a darkened tunnel. Fallen brown leaves covered the pavement. There were houses along the way, built on large swaths of property, which kept the neighboring houses at a distance.

Rand followed the highlighted route down the curvy pathway on the GPS, the tension inside him growing as he neared.

The blue line ran out. "You have arrived at your destination," the GPS announced.

When Rand slowed to a stop, he saw only darkness. He turned the Jeep and drove into the lot to point his high beams, confirming what he feared.

No driveway. No house. The address was for an empty lot of overgrown grass and dead leaves.

Rand grabbed the flashlight and got out of the car and looked around. Miller followed his lead while the girls waited behind.

There was a house, 811 Plaster Road, to his left. The next, presumably 815, was off in the distance. The lot between them was large enough for a house, and had probably contained 813 at some point. But now it was gone.

"This can't be happening," Rand muttered.

"The demonic are experts at these kinds of tricks," Miller said. The bright headlights cast long, ominous shadows on the leaf-covered ground.

Rand's headache was growing worse. "A dead end."

"Not yet," Miller said. "Let's at least have a look around. Maybe there's something we can discover here."

The two men walked farther onto the property, the leaves crunching underneath their shoes. Rand swept his flashlight around the area, looking for anything.

"No trees," he said. "That means this lot was cleared,

and the house was probably here at some point. But it's not anymore."

"Wonder why," Miller said.

"This has to mean something," Rand said, as if trying to force it to be true. "All the houses on Plaster Road are still intact, right? Except this address. The odd factor is always what we should consider."

"I guess," Miller said. "But again, what does it mean?"

Then he heard it, coming from the darkness to his left.

The loud clicks of someone cocking a shotgun.

23

Miller's hands shot up toward the sky, a knee-jerk reaction. Rand followed suit, still holding the flashlight. He froze, but out of the corner of his, he could make out the shadow of a man who was pointing the barrel of his shotgun right at them.

"Hey, take it easy, we're not here to hurt you," Rand said.

"I finally caught you, you son of a bitch."

"You have the wrong guy," Rand said.

"Wrong guy, huh?" The man spoke with a thick southern accent. "I don't think so."

"I'm here to help you."

"Here's what we're gonna do," the man said. "I'm calling the police, and you're not gonna move until they get here. I'm sick of all the commotion you're causin' and I won't stand for it anymore, so you'd better not move, or else—"

"You can't shoot us," Miller said. "This technically isn't your property. Property defense doesn't apply here."

The man shifted his gun to Miller and he fell silent.

"You there," the man said to Rand. "You live around here? I don't recognize you."

"I don't," Rand said. "I've been dealing with some pests who've led me here. If you put down your gun, we can talk about this and get to the bottom of it."

The man considered his words for a few moments, then lowered his gun. Rand and Miller dropped their hands.

The man stepped forward and the bright beam from Rand's flashlight revealed him. He was old, perhaps in his seventies, and wore boots, tan cargo pants, and a loose-fitting, button-down shirt with his long sleeves rolled over his forearm. His face was wrinkled and stern.

"Name's Randolph Casey. Friends call me Rand." He held out his hand, and the man shook it.

"Wayne Swanson."

"This is Miller." Miller opted not to shake, but lifted his palm in an awkward wave, seemingly still dazed from the close call.

Footsteps rustled the dead leaves on the ground. Rand shined his light—Libby and Stacy rushed over to him.

"Is everything okay?" Libby asked.

"Everything's fine now," Rand answered for Wayne, hoping to force that narrative. "Everyone was just a little spooked, which is understandable, since it's late and we're not supposed to be here. But it's all good. Wayne, this is my daughter Libby."

"What you folks doing here in the middle of the night?" Wayne asked. "You picked the wrong place to poke around. I almost blasted y'all."

"We're interested in this house," Rand said. "Eight-one-three Plaster Road. Except it doesn't seem to be here anymore."

"Interested? Why?"

"Long story, my friend. We've been chasing down some nasty Halloween pranksters. Wanted to teach them a lesson, you know. Talk to their parents and tell them what their kids were up to. We thought this was where they lived, but as you can see…"

In most of Rand's cases, there always seemed to come a time when he needed help from a third party. He didn't like to lie to these people about what he was doing, but it was useful to leave out the "hard-to-believe" details. If he began every conversation disclosing he was a demonologist and paranormal investigator, he'd never get very far.

"Maybe you and I have the same nuisance," Wayne said.

"What problems have you been having?"

"Well…" Wayne adjusted his cap. "Truth is, I don't know. Trespassers, but they're real slippery. Can't seem to corner 'em."

"What do you mean?" Rand asked.

"Past couple weeks, they been showin' up. I'll take the dog out at night before me and Geraldine head to bed, and then Boss will spot 'em. They usually stand in this lot, right around there." He pointed. "Sometimes in those trees. Man, Boss goes nuts. Barkin', hollerin', slobberin' everywhere. But he won't go over, which is weird, 'cause Boss ain't usually afraid of no one."

Rand and Miller exchanged a glance.

"Did you ever see what these guys looked like?" Miller asked.

"Nope. They always standin' in the dark, and they run

off before I can get a look at 'em. I called the cops a few times and they check around, but they never find nothin'. They won't come out anymore, 'cause now they think crazy old Wayne is seein' things."

Libby looked worried, as did Miller. Rand knew what was going on. There was definitely supernatural activity in this area, and Wayne was catching glimpses. While that definitely wasn't good for Wayne, it meant progress for Rand.

The vacant lot was not the dead end he'd thought it was.

"What's the deal with this place?" Rand said. "What happened to the house?"

"Oh yeah," Wayne said. "This was where the Erlich family lived."

"Who are the Erlichs?"

Wayne stared at him. "You serious? The Erlich family murders from 1984?"

"I would have been seven years old in 1984," Rand said.

"Ah. Either way, no one seems to remember that except for me and Geraldine. Maybe 'cause I lived here this whole time, so it's impossible to forget."

"What happened?"

"The Erlichs were my neighbors. They had a daughter and she had two young kids, each from a different fella. That girl had a boyfriend who was the father of neither, and one night he went crazy and broke in and shot all of 'em, then himself. I heard the shots and called the police. But by the time they got here, it was all said and done."

"Oh my God," Libby whispered under her breath.

"That sounds familiar," Miller said. "Pretty sure I read

about it somewhere. One of the worst crimes in the city's history."

"It was," Wayne said. "They were a nice family, if a bit messy with the lawn upkeep. Those two kids always had their toys in the yard. Anyway, that doesn't mean they deserved what happened to 'em. Tragic shame, really."

"So what about the house?" Rand asked.

"Well, as you can imagine, no one wanted to live there after that, and I don't blame 'em. The place started to fall apart. If I ever had a moment, I'd go in there and fix up some things, but time went on, I got older, and it became too much. It eventually turned into an eyesore, so I wrote to the city council to do something about it, but they don't pay any attention to us folks way out here on Plaster.

"Anyway, about two years ago, I heard someone had purchased the land. Probably got it for a steal. I figured they would show up and assess the place, but they didn't for the longest time, until one day men showed up with their bulldozers. Said the new owner wanted the house demolished. I watched as they tore it all down. Good riddance."

"Any idea who bought the property?" Rand asked.

Wayne only shrugged. "Not the foggiest."

Rand had not even lived in the city in 1984, so he'd never heard of the Erlich family murders. However, an event like that was sure to leave behind a huge surge of negative energy. Honestly, Rand was surprised that Wayne hadn't experienced anything strange until only recently.

The daughter had two young boys, Rand thought.

"So I don't know," Wayne said. "Only thing I can figure is someone's picked up on this spot and wrote about it or somethin'. You know these true crime books and these podcast things? Murderers and tragedies—folks eat that stuff up nowadays. Boggles me. But anyway, maybe some nuts want to see the place. Whoever bought it should set it up as a tourist attraction. But I hope he does somethin' soon, because these people are drivin' me crazy and upsettin' my dog."

"I'm sorry all this is happening to you," Rand said. "But I think I can help."

"How? And why?" Wayne's eyes narrowed, and Rand could see the realization dawn on him. "Oh... You're one those nuts, aren't you? Which are you? Murderer fan or ghost hunter?"

Rand let the question linger for a moment before he answered, trying to decide his best course of action. He figured he'd developed enough of a rapport with Wayne by then to go with the truth. "Ghost hunter."

Wayne scoffed. "I don't know which is worse."

"This is why I can help you. The things you're seeing—"

Wayne waved his hand at him. "Don't even start with me. My wife Geraldine's the one who believes in all that spirit nonsense, not me."

"I was serious when I said I had the same problems as you. I have intruders that always vanish, and I think this place has something to do with them."

Wayne rubbed his forehead and adjusted his cap again. "Look, you seem like a nice guy, but I ain't about to get into it with you. I wish you'd just leave."

"Give us the rest of the night," Rand said. "I want to search more around here. After tonight, I won't come back, and you'll never see me again. But if I find what I'm looking for, you'll stop having trespassers on your property."

Wayne looked at him and sighed. "Whatever, man. If you wanna waste your time, go ahead. But I'll take you up on your offer. If I catch you here again after tonight, I'll call the police."

"Deal. Also, if anyone knocks on your door tonight, don't answer it. And definitely don't let anyone inside. Just please trust me on that."

Wayne eyed them all in turn, clearly skeptical. "You folks have yourselves a good night." The leaves crunched under his boots as he headed back to his house.

"Charming guy," Miller muttered.

"A bad tragedy happened here," Stacy said, "and that's what attracts the spirits and negative energy. Just like what you teach us in class." Rand nodded. "He said the family had two boys."

"Exactly."

"But what does that have to do with Kim?"

"That's the part I have to figure out." Rand swept his flashlight across the empty lot. There was nothing but dead leaves and broken sticks covering the ground.

"You have less than five hours to do it, Rando," Miller said, checking his watch.

"Dad," Libby said. She held her buzzing phone. "Mom's calling. She's probably home and wondering where I am."

"Let her know."

Libby answered and took a few steps away to speak to Tessa.

"So what do we do?" Miller asked.

"It's obvious that something is going on here," Rand said. "This lot is a hotbed of spiritual activity, and I got the address straight from the black-eyed kids. It's all connected somehow."

He already knew the best solution when he needed to uncover what was hidden from the naked eye.

"I need to bring in a medium."

24

Wayne closed the door behind him, glad to shut out the midnight chill and the crazies that had wandered onto the empty lot next door.

"Lunatics," he muttered as he walked toward the closet near the back door to drop off his shotgun.

A figure stood in the center of the living room. Wayne let out a yelp and leapt back, instinctively grabbing his shotgun into both hands. Only after a moment did he realize it was Geraldine.

"You gonna shoot me now, Wayne?" His wife placed her hands on her hips.

"What the hell are you doin' standin' around in the dark like that?" Wayne barked, heart pounding from the sudden fright. "I thought you went to bed."

"I'm trying to figure out why you're running around the neighbor's property in the middle of the night."

"We ain't got no neighbors."

Geraldine clicked on a lamp. "Seriously, Wayne. What's going on?"

Wayne jabbed his thumb over his shoulder. "There's some nut jobs outside. Paranormal seekers or some such."

Geraldine had appeared annoyed, but now her face softened. "Really? What do they want?"

Wayne sighed. He really should have been more careful with his words. "Nothin'"

"What do they want, Wayne?" Geraldine said.

Wayne adjusted his cap, really not in the mood to talk about it. "They're interested in the Erlichs."

Wayne avoided talking about the family that used to live next door. His wife had become attached to the two boys. She'd always wanted children, but it had never happened for them, so those two had filled that void.

Geraldine still carried the pain of losing the Erlich children to such a horrific crime. Many years had passed since then, but something had changed in Geraldine that night, and that broken piece of her had never been the same.

"Do they know something about the boys?" Geraldine asked, a hopeful hint behind her voice.

Wayne had to be gentle here, yet firm. When it came to the two boys next door, Geraldine never thought sensibly. "Let those people do what they need to do so they can leave. Ain't no sense getting involved."

"But Wayne—"

There came three knocks on the front door.

Wayne whirled around. He couldn't believe it. "Are they *seriously* bangin' on my door? I already told 'em everythin' I knew."

"Let them in," Geraldine said.

Wayne glanced back at his wife. "You crazy?"

"It's cold out there, Wayne," she said. "Let them inside."

Wayne muttered a curse under his breath. The last thing he wanted was Geraldine meeting paranormal nuts. His wife was already a half-step away from being one of them herself, what with all the spirituality books she read and ghost hunting TV programs she watched.

I'll just shoo 'em away, Wayne thought. *There's nothin' else I can tell them anyhow.*

Wayne opened the door, expecting to see the ghost-hunting man and his heavyset friend. But there, standing on his porch, were two young boys.

Wayne took a startled step backwards. They resembled the two boys that used to live next door.

No, Wayne thought. *This is impossible. They've been dead for years.*

The pair looked like they hadn't had a bath in a fortnight and wore summer clothes even thought it was cold outside. Wayne wondered why they weren't wearing any shoes.

Wayne tried to speak, but his voice only came out as a dry croak. The two boys stared into the house without looking at him.

"We need to use your telegraph," the older boy said.

"Pardon?" Wayne finally managed to say. Wayne was old, but even he hadn't ever seen a telegraph machine.

"Who is it?" Geraldine called behind him. "Is it the paranormal guy?"

Wayne heard Geraldine's bare feet on the floor as she began to walk toward him, but a strong instinct seized his gut, one that he couldn't explain.

"Don't come any closer, Geraldine," Wayne shouted.

"We aren't going to hurt you." The older boy spoke louder now, angry. "We just need to come inside and use your telegraph. We're only two young children, so you can trust us."

Wayne did not like the way the kids were speaking to him. Rudeness aside, something was giving him a very adverse feeling to their presence. A horrible stench had also risen to his nose.

Somethin' ain't right, he thought.

Geraldine gasped, suddenly beside Wayne. He hadn't heard his wife walk up to the door.

"It's them," she whispered.

"Let us in!" the older boy shouted.

"Get out of their way, Wayne," Geraldine said, gripping his arm. "They must be freezing."

Wayne was not one to believe in anything supernatural, and these two boys were not an exception. But he now remembered that the paranormal nut had warned him not to answer the door if anyone came knocking, nor to let anyone in.

And despite everything else that raced through Wayne's mind, his horrible gut feeling took over. He slammed the door in the kids' faces, feeling instant relief the moment they were out of sight.

"What are you doing, Wayne?" Geraldine cried. "Have you lost your mind?"

Geraldine shoved Wayne out of the way and opened the front door again.

The front porch was empty.

Geraldine fell silent and walked out onto the porch. Wayne readied his gun and stood close behind her. The two of them scanned the dark front yard.

"Where did they go?" Geraldine shivered.

There hadn't been enough time for the two boys to walk away that fast. It seemed they'd simply vanished into thin air.

"Wayne, what's going on?" Geraldine asked, her voice more hesitant now.

"I don't know," he said. "But if that paranormal nut comes back later, I'll have a thing or two to say to him."

25

Tessa had reclined her car seat and was hoping to doze off, but it was too uncomfortable. The clock on the dashboard read 1:36 AM. She couldn't wait to change out of her witch costume, wash off all her makeup, and crawl into her king-sized bed. Bill drove. He still wore the bolts in his neck from his low-effort Frankenstein Halloween costume.

"You okay?" Bill asked as he turned into the neighborhood.

"Just tired."

Tessa had been to a few parties for Southern Finance, Bill's company. "Party" was hardly the word to describe them. Bill's employees and colleagues were all nice enough, but not exactly thrilling. They discussed work, difficult clients and industry trends while Tessa would simply nod and smile and be supportive.

Life with Bill was quiet, but good. Structured and stable. A far cry from her past relationship. Their wedding was in a few months, and Tessa was looking forward to solidifying her new life.

"Did you have fun?"

"Yeah," she said, although her voice spiked up, which happened whenever she told a white lie.

"Good. Me too."

Bill was never much for reading between the lines.

"You were right," Bill went on. "The Halloween party was a good idea. I didn't believe they'd be into it, but they were. Some of those costumes were wild, don't you think?"

"Yeah." In truth, everyone's costumes were basic. Creative dressing was not in these peoples' skill set. Costumes and parties weren't numbers or sales or interest rates. But at least they'd tried.

"And did you hear Terry tell that story about his client in Indonesia?" Bill started laughing all over again. Tessa had heard it, but hadn't understood all its technicalities or why it was funny.

Bill pulled into the empty driveway, and Tessa shot up straight, alarmed. "Where's Libby's car? She's not here."

"Umm..." Bill struggled to put words together. "I'm sure she's fine."

Tessa fished her phone from her purse. No missed calls or text messages. She unlocked it and dialed her daughter's number. As it rang, she threw off her seatbelt and left the car.

"Hey, Mom," Libby answered.

"Are you okay? I just got home and you're not here. You said you'd be back before midnight."

"Yeah, I'm fine."

"What's going on? Where are you? Who are you with?"

175

Libby hesitated. "I'm with Dad."

Bill stood with Tessa in the driveway as she talked, looking on worriedly.

"With your dad? How did that happen?" she asked. Bill furrowed his brow in confusion.

"There's been an incident."

That word. It had been the same one Rand had used earlier that day when he'd barged into the house. Tessa had dismissed it then, but now she could hear how serious Libby was. "What do you mean?"

"It's kind of a long story, but I can tell you about it later."

"No!" Tessa barked. "Libby, you need to come home right this instant." She headed up the driveway and toward the front door. Bill followed.

"But Mom—"

"I don't want you involved in whatever your dad is doing. Not after what happened last time."

"What's going on?" Bill asked, but Tessa didn't answer him.

"I'm with Dad. I'm safe," Libby pleaded.

"Do you have your car? I'm coming to get you if you don't. Where are you? Where's Bailey and your other friends?"

"Mom." Libby's eye roll could be heard in her voice, and that infuriated Tessa even more.

"Put your father on."

"Hang on."

Bill unlocked and opened the front door and he and Tessa went inside. The living room was warm and the outside chill melted off.

"Tess," Rand said.

"What the *hell* do you think you're doing?"

"I could say the same thing to you. You allowed her out of the house, and now something's happened."

"I am so *sick* of his crap, Rand. Where are you? Are you going to bring her here, or should I come there?"

"Let me call you back in five minutes and we can figure out how to get her home," Rand said.

"No. I want to help you, Dad," came Libby's voice in the background.

"I swear, Randolph, if you hang up this phone—"

Bill closed the door behind her. As soon as he did, someone knocked.

Tessa paused. Bill gave her a confused look.

"Did you see anyone when we were out there?" Bill asked.

For a moment, Tessa forgot about Rand. "No. Did you?"

Bill shook his head. "Must be some late-night trick-or-treaters. Why are they out at this time? I'll get rid of them."

"Are you talking to me or Bill?" Rand asked.

"Bill," Tessa said, turning her attention back to the conversation. "Someone just knocked."

"Seriously? Tessa, don't—"

The line went dead. When she checked the screen, the empty battery indicator flashed.

That's weird. She'd known her phone battery was low, but not enough to die on her.

Bill opened the door. Two young children were on the doorstep. One was a head taller than the other and they were dressed similarly in shorts and t-shirts. For some strange reason... they were barefoot.

When Tessa saw them, she recoiled, though she couldn't pinpoint why. Something about them was *very* off.

"We need to come in and use your telephone," the oldest boy said.

Even the way he spoke was wrong. It was too clear, too precise, as if there was a ventriloquist standing off to the side, speaking for him.

"Umm..." Bill glanced back at Tessa, then to the kids. "Where are your parents? Are you okay?"

"We only need to come in and use your telephone. We're just two kids and we aren't going to hurt you."

An overwhelming sense of foreboding swirled through Tessa's body. It was a feeling she had not felt in a long time, but she remembered it well. She felt it during the years she was with Rand, when the monsters from his cases paid her little visits.

There's been an incident, he'd said.

"I guess that would be all right," Bill said. "You can call your parents and wait here until they come to pick you up."

Since she was frozen in fear, it took Tessa a few moments to realize what Bill had just said. Her instinct seized control. She bolted toward the door and slammed it shut in the kids' faces.

"What are you doing?" Bill looked at her like she'd gone nuts. Maybe she had.

"Don't let them in," she said.

"What are you talking about? They're kids and they need our help."

"No. I have a terrible feeling about them. And Rand said—"

"Come on, Tess." Bill gave her an exasperated look. "How many times do I have to tell you. You can't let Rand keep getting in your head. You're *free* from that now."

"This is different, Bill. Those kids aren't right."

Bill regarded her for a moment before choosing to ignore her and open the door again. But when he did, the two kids were gone.

He walked out onto the porch and looked around the yard. Then, he came back in confused. "They sure walk fast."

They vanished, Tessa thought. *The yard is way too big for them to get out of sight that quickly.*

"Well, I hope they get home," Bill said, closing the door again.

As soon as he did, there were another three knocks.

Bill backed away from the door. Tessa grabbed his arm and squeezed it.

"What in the world?" he whispered.

"Don't answer it."

They waited, staring at the door in silence. A minute later, three more knocks, louder than the ones before.

Bill stiffened beside her. "Will they go away?" he asked.

"I think so."

Tessa heard footsteps on the other side of the door. It sounded like the two kids were rapidly pacing back and forth.

Then their footsteps started stamping *on* the door as if they were kicking it. Then continued up the length of the door.

Tessa realized the two kids were walking *up* the door.

The steps continued along the outside wall of the house. Tessa and Bill followed the sounds with their eyes.

The kids reached the roof. Tessa went to the kitchen in the back of the house, following them. Bill was right behind her.

The two sets of footsteps traversed the entire roof and began their steady climb down the opposite wall. They walked down the rear side of the house and halted just outside the back door of the kitchen.

A moment later, there came another three knocks.

"How do we get rid of them?" Bill whispered.

"Go away!" Tessa shouted at them.

Three more pounds, harder than before, which rattled the door on its hinges.

"Leave us alone."

Another strike, this one sounding like a battering ram. The door shook and the wood cracked. Tessa and Bill leapt back, startled.

The house fell silent again.

Bill had his arm around Tessa, and in that moment she wondered which of the two of them were more afraid.

"I think they're gone," Tessa whispered after the silence had lingered.

"Are you sure?"

She removed herself from Bill's embrace and inched toward the door, holding her breath.

"Don't open it," Bill said.

There was only one way to be sure. She gripped the knob, working up her courage, and then flung the door open.

No one was there. The outside surface of the door had been bashed in, the paint chipped and cracked.

Bill joined Tessa and inspected the door. It would have

taken a huge force to cause that kind of damage. No kid was strong enough to do that.

The silence broke sharply when Bill's cell phone rang. He glanced at the screen, then answered. "Hey, Rand." He listened. "Actually, no, everything is not okay. I think you should come over."

26

For the first time in a long while, Rand felt overwhelmed. He just couldn't keep up.

He sped through town in his Jeep, Miller and Libby and Stacy riding with him. It seemed like the more he dug into solving the mystery, the more the black-eyed kids attacked. They were spreading their reach, forcing Rand to stretch himself thin as he addressed each event.

When he got to Bill's house, Bill and Tessa were waiting on the expansive front porch. Tessa wore jeans and a sweatshirt, but still had on the black lipstick that Rand had caught her wearing earlier. Bill's thinning black hair was standing on end and he'd forgotten to remove the plastic bolts from his neck that Rand assumed had been part of a Frankenstein costume.

Tessa rushed to Libby and hugged her. "Are you okay? Oh my God, what happened to your arm?"

"I'm fine, Mom."

Bill was paler than usual. "What happened here?" Rand asked him.

"Come see."

Rand followed Bill into the kitchen and to the back door where he showed him the damage. It looked like a cannonball had been fired into the door.

"They came to the front door first. You were on the phone with Tess, and the phone died just after they knocked. I was about to let them in, but Tess got a really bad feeling from them, so she slammed the door on them. When I opened it up again, they were gone."

Rand was relieved. Tessa had developed a sense for evil entities when they had been together—it was almost inevitable for anyone who dated him for long enough. Seems like it had served her well here.

"They knocked again, but I didn't answer. After that, they climbed straight up the door and wall and onto the roof, then down this wall here." Bill pointed as he explained. "They were right outside the back door. When they realized we weren't going to answer, they gave it one last pound before leaving us alone. That's where this damage came from."

Rand grew sick as he listened. "This is what I've been dealing with all night. They're popping up everywhere. You did the right thing by not letting them in."

"I almost did," Bill said. "Tessa stopped me at the last second. She said they didn't feel right."

I taught her well, Rand thought.

Rand and Bill returned to the living room, where everyone gathered. Stacy, Miller, Libby, and Tessa. All eyes turned to him, weary and frightened and confused, all waiting for him to guide them.

It was nearing three o'clock in the morning, and the adrenaline spikes Rand had been experiencing all night were fading. His mind was foggy, his focus torn in many directions. He wanted to stop, regroup and reassess, but there was no time. He *needed* to figure this out before sunrise—Shindael had promised that Kim's life depended on it.

"What does it mean, Rand?" Tessa asked him. "What are these things, and what do they want?"

"They want us," Rand said. "As far as I know. They've already taken Stacy's friend."

"Where did they take her?"

"Long explanation, but it has something to do with an empty lot on Plaster Road." He glanced at Miller. "As I said before Tessa called, I think the best course of action is to bring in a medium."

Miller nodded. "I agree. But that means…"

Rand sighed. *It means I have to call Katie.*

She was the only medium he knew in town, but she'd stopped working with Rand when the pressure of always communicating with the other side had gotten to be too much.

"I promised to not call her for any more cases," Rand said.

"What other option do you have?" Miller asked him. "You have to try."

Miller was right. Rand glanced at Libby, who shrugged in agreement.

He took out his phone and brought up her number from his list of contacts. She would be furious that he was waking her up.

The phone rang and rang, not going to voice mail. Everyone watched Rand as he waited for her to pick up.

He was about to hang up when her familiar voice answered. "Rand?"

"Katie. Hey. Sorry to call so late."

"What do you want?" Her tone was guarded and skeptical.

"There's been an incident." It was quickly becoming his motto for the evening.

"Are you okay?"

"Listen… a case has come up."

"You promised me that we were finished. I'm out of it."

"I know, but…"

"We've talked about this," she said. "My world is different these days, and I like it. The last time we worked together was my worst experience by far."

Rand remembered that well. It was only a short while ago the demon Karax had wreaked havoc through St. Mary's Medical Center.

"I know, Katie, and I'm sorry, but—"

"Besides, even if I wanted to help you, I couldn't. I'm not in town."

"Oh."

"I'm in New York City with Mitch. He's here for business and he invited me along. I won't be back for another week."

That was definitely a problem. He needed her now.

"Right. Sorry to bother you."

"Good luck, Rand. I understand it's not easy."

"It never is." He hung up the phone and faced the roomful of people who were counting on him to figure something out. "She isn't in town."

"So what do we do?" Miller asked.

"I don't know." He looked at his daughter, but she only stared at the ground, looking lost in thought.

"Maybe you can try to do it yourself," Miller said.

"I'm not sensitive enough," Rand said. "I've tried before."

"Yeah, but what other option do you have? You're running out of time."

"You've told us before in class you sometimes see and communicate with the spiritual world," Stacy said.

"That's true, but usually only by accident. It's not something I'm able to turn on and off at will, like an experienced medium."

"Can you please try?" Stacy begged.

"The empty lot definitely has spiritual activity," Rand said, "but when we were there, I couldn't perceive it."

"But—"

"Dad," Libby spoke up. Everyone looked at her. "I…"

"What?" Rand asked.

"I think I know someone who can help."

27

W hat came out of Libby's mouth was the last thing Rand had expected to hear.

"Georgia?" Rand said, and she nodded. "What are you talking about?"

"She called me earlier today," Libby said. She looked like she was making a troubling confession. "She planned to talk to you about this, but wanted to tell me first. I met her at St. Mary's and she admitted that she sees spirits now. Not like the demon from last time," she added quickly. "But, you know, benign spirits. Ones of people who passed away at the hospital, or used to work there a long time ago."

"Seriously?" Rand asked. His daughter nodded. He rubbed at his temples and closed his eyes.

He never liked learning that someone had begun experiencing the spiritual world, much less someone he knew. As much as he hated to admit it, Georgia seeing spirits made perfect sense to Rand. Georgia was terminally ill, and those close to death were often more in tune with the spiritual world that was normally invisible to most people.

Plus, Georgia had had a recent brush with spiritual warfare. All of those factors combined were very likely to make her sensitive.

"Why didn't she tell me?" Rand asked.

"She was going to," Libby said. "But I suggested she wait until after Halloween, since you were being your usual crazy self."

"I don't think Georgia will understand the seriousness of this."

"I tried to explain it to her, but she told me she wanted to embrace it," Libby said. "She saw the way you and Katie helped her, and she was hoping she could use this ability to also help other people."

"Absolutely not." Tessa stepped in between Rand and Libby. "You will *not* bring this girl into your mess."

"I actually agree," Rand said. "Georgia shouldn't get involved in this."

"But Dad, what else are you going to do?" Libby said. "There's no other option."

"There has to be," Tessa said.

"Even if she wants to embrace being sensitive, she is untrained and inexperienced," Rand said. "And these beings we've encountered tonight are very powerful. It isn't safe."

"No," Tessa said. "She *won't* embrace being sensitive, she *won't* get involved with your shenanigans, and you will not—"

Libby brushed past her Mom, stepping closer to Rand. "There's something going on in that empty lot. You can't figure it out on your own. You always used to call in

Katie, but now she can't come. What else can you do if you don't call Georgia?"

"Libby," Tessa chastised.

Rand sighed. His daughter was right. He was in a corner and out of options. He glanced at Miller, who only shrugged. Then he looked to Stacy, who only watched him pleadingly, begging him to conjure up some sort of plan.

"She already told me that this was something she wanted," Libby said. "If you ask her, she'll try to help you."

He checked his watch. It was very late—or early in the morning—but he knew Georgia had a habit of staying up well into the night.

"Call her," Rand finally said.

As Libby pulled out her phone and stepped into the kitchen to place the call, Tessa rushed over to Rand and shoved his shoulder. "You are unbelievable. How many people do you have to expose to this insanity?"

"We're desperate right now, Tessa."

Bill put a hand on Tessa's arm as she continued to glare at Rand. Libby returned to the living room and held out her cell toward Rand. He took the phone and hesitated for a moment, reconsidering if he truly wanted to go down this road. He didn't, but he needed to.

"Hey, Georgia."

"Happy Halloween, Ghost Man." Despite the late hour, she sounded chipper. The familiar voice would have made him smile under normal circumstances.

"What are you still doing up?" Rand asked.

"Are you serious? It's Halloween night and *all* the good movies are on. I just watched *The Texas Chainsaw Massacre* and *Child's Play*. I'm not going to sleep for a week. Why do I do this to myself?"

"You're a brave girl," Rand said.

"I know. So, Libby told me she told you what I told her." She paused. "Did you get that? I confused myself."

"I got it. Do you realize this is very serious?"

"Yes. Libby said you're in the middle of a situation right now. Kind of like what happened to me."

"Similar, but different. I need Katie, but she's out of town."

"So I'm your second string."

"I don't want you to be. This would be a huge burden for you to take on."

"But I owe you, Ghost Man. You saved my life."

"You don't owe me anything for that."

"I'm fifteen, so I'm practically an adult, which means I can decide for myself."

"Fifteen isn't even close to being an adult."

"Wrong. You know about dog years, right? When a dog is six, they say he's forty in dog years. I get to do the same thing because of my disease. So really, I'm the same age as you."

Rand had to chuckle. Georgia's short life expectancy saddened him, but the girl handled it well, all things considered.

"Besides," she went on, more serious. "I told Libby this, and I'll tell you too. I want to use the time I have left to help people. There isn't much they let a fifteen-year-old do, because adults don't understand the concept of dog years, so maybe this is my thing. If I have this ability, I may as well embrace it."

Even though Rand wanted to shelter Georgia from the

spiritual world, it was hard to argue with her line of thinking. "Where are your parents right now?" he asked.

"They're at home. I'm at the hospital."

"Can you leave?"

"You remember Harold the security guard? He'll allow me out. Especially if I tell him I'm going to see you. He likes you a lot, and he always asks me when you're coming to visit."

"After this is over, I promise I'll drop by and visit both you and him. Let him know."

"Cool. So, are you picking me up? Where are we going? What are we doing? Is it another demon?"

"I'll send Libby to get you. She'll explain everything on the way."

"Sounds good, Ghost Man."

"Be sure to dress warm. It's cold out there."

She hung up and Rand gave the phone back to Libby. "Take your mother's car and grab Georgia. Then meet me at the empty lot."

"So now you're helping yourself to our vehicles?" Tessa folded her arms.

Rand noticed that Stacy was no longer in the room. "Wait... where's Stacy?"

Bill pointed toward the front door. "She went outside while you were on the phone. She seemed upset."

Rand hadn't seen her leave. "Right. I'll talk to her."

"Mom," Libby said, holding out her hand. "Can I borrow your keys? Please?"

Tessa stared at her daughter in disbelief. "Why do you insist on staying involved? You remember what happened last time. You were *kidnapped*."

"Yeah, it's dangerous and scary, but what you don't see

is that Dad helps a lot of people who wouldn't know what to do if he wasn't there for them. I've seen these monsters, and you have too. They're really bad, and they hurt people. They have to be stopped. We both know Dad is the only one who can do it."

Tessa eyed the rips in Libby's sleeves and the red gashes on her skin. She didn't budge, apparently unmoved by her daughter's speech.

Bill dropped his own keys into Libby's hand. "Promise to come home if things get too out of control."

Tessa glared at Bill, incredulous.

"Thanks, Bill." Libby rushed out the house before anyone could stop her.

"I can't believe you," Tessa rounded on Bill. He started to explain himself, but Tessa spoke over him, drowning out his excuses.

Rand eyed Miller, who frowned at him. "Any other suggestions before Libby springs a cystic fibrosis teenager from the hospital in the middle of the night so she can speak to spirits?"

"You're doing the best you can with what you have."

Rand went outside onto Bill's front porch. He found Stacy sitting on the steps, staring into the night. Libby was backing Bill's BMW out of the driveway onto the street.

Rand lowered himself next to Stacy. Under the porch light, he could see she'd been crying again.

"Is your daughter going to get that girl?" Stacy asked.

"Yes."

Stacy grimaced. Rand assumed she blamed herself for another person getting roped into her situation.

"I'm the one bringing Georgia into this," Rand said,

trying to shift the responsibility onto himself. Stacy didn't respond. She wasn't buying it. "How are you holding up?"

The question made Stacy sniff, threatening to bring on a fresh wave of new tears. "This is all my fault."

"You can't say that," Rand said. "It isn't true."

"But it is," Stacy said. "They came for me that first night. If I had just done more to make Kim understand what they were, then she would've known to not let them in. She didn't take me seriously, and I should have insisted."

"You're thinking about it too much," Rand said. "You can't predict what someone will do, especially when the supernatural is involved."

Stacy wiped away a tear that escaped her eye. "Even if that's true, *I* was the one who invited them to the house."

"What do you mean?" Rand asked.

"It finally dawned on me when you were on the phone with that girl. You always repeated the most important rule about dark spirits. If you invite them, they will come. I studied and obsessed over your class just like all my other ones. I mean, I read about this stuff every day. I thought about it when I wasn't studying. I even dreamed about it sometimes. After all that, *of course* I was inviting them."

"This will be all over soon," Rand said, hoping it was true. "We'll get Kim back."

Stacy looked at him, eyes still wet. He could read the silent question on her face.

What if we don't?

In Rand's experience, that was never something to consider.

"We'll be strong," he said. "We'll fight hard."

28

L ibby drove into the familiar parking garage and glided Bill's BMW, smooth and seamless, into one of the many spots by the hospital entrance. The empty garage was vast, capable of housing the cars of all the visitors that St. Mary's welcomed during the day. But now, Libby felt alone and isolated.

She took out her phone and tapped out a text to Georgia. The clicking from the phone's touch screen keyboard was loud against the silence.

"Hey, I'm here in the garage. Do you want to meet me here?"

Three dots appeared as Georgia typed back.

"Sure. Be there in a minute."

As Libby waited in the idling car, the parking garage seemed to grow dimmer, as if not all the lights were being used. There were a few other cars, but they were parked far from where she was. She couldn't see anyone else around.

She thought there was movement in the rearview

mirror. She glanced up, but the shape zipped out of view in the reflection. Libby twisted in her seat and looked over her shoulder.

Maybe it had been her imagination. Libby couldn't see anyone else in the parking garage, though she no longer felt that she was alone. She didn't want to be there anymore.

Libby took her phone out and sent another text to Georgia.

"Actually, I'm coming in. Meet you by the main elevator."

She got out of the car and hurried inside the hospital.

The expansive lobby was devoid of personnel. Only an elderly volunteer sat at the desk, and she put her book down and straightened in her chair as if expecting Libby to ask for directions. Libby avoided eye contact and continued down the main corridor.

When she reached the elevator, it dinged and opened, and Georgia came out before Libby could go in. She wore jeans and a zipped-up hoodie, her blonde hair tied up in a messy bun on the back of her head.

"I thought you were waiting for me in the car," Georgia said. She rolled her portable oxygen cylinder behind her, the clear plastic nasal cannula dangling from her nostrils.

"I got freaked out," Libby admitted.

"You look terrible," Georgia said.

"It's been a long night."

Georgia eyed the three gashes in Libby's sleeve. Although they had stopped bleeding, her blood still marred the camouflage pattern. "I guess this is what we're dealing with."

"Before we go," Libby said, "I just want to make sure you've given this plenty of thought. This is all happening very fast, and you haven't had a lot of time to really consider."

"I'm sure," Georgia said. "As a matter of fact, I feel like I didn't get a fair fight last time. That demon just possessed me and your dad had to save me. *Now* I have a chance to take one on for real."

"This isn't a game," Libby said.

Georgia grabbed Libby's hand and pulled her along down the hallway. "Come on, let's get moving."

A few minutes later, they passed the hospital's chapel, and Libby froze. The memories came back to her. Not that long ago, the demon Karax had chased her and Georgia through those same corridors. He'd cornered them in the chapel, which he could not enter. That was when Georgia had collapsed in Libby's arms, and when Georgia woke up, Karax had possessed her.

"You okay?" Georgia asked.

"Maybe we should pray before we go," Libby said. Her dad always tried to pray before taking on the demonic.

"I thought we didn't have time." Georgia paused, then said, "Actually, you're right."

She flung open the chapel doors and marched inside. It resembled a miniature church, with pews on either side of a carpeted aisle and an altar at the front. The place had been repaired since Karax had destroyed it. Libby remembered how the demon had turned the entire chapel to rubble in the span of a few seconds.

Georgia approached the altar and took the cross that was there.

"Stealing from the chapel?" Libby asked.

"Father Calvin won't mind if we *borrow* this for the night."

Georgia was right. Any kind of religious icon was a defense against the demonic.

When they returned the parking garage, Libby noticed it had grown even darker. A shiver went up her spine, and it wasn't from the chilly night.

"This place gives me the creeps when it's empty," Georgia said.

"Come on. Let's get out of here."

They got into the car, but when Libby turned the key the ignition wouldn't start.

"Oh, no." She tried again, but the battery only clicked.

"Did you leave the headlights on or something?" Georgia asked.

"No. And even if I did, I wasn't inside long enough to kill the battery."

Libby realized what was going on. She knew it even before the shadow darted across the rearview mirror.

She and Georgia saw it at the same time and simultaneously looked behind them through the back window.

Nothing.

"Did you see that?" Georgia whispered.

"Yes."

"Try to start the car again."

Libby twisted the key again and again. The engine struggled to turn over, and the lights on the dashboard dimly blinked, searching for a source of power from the battery.

"Come on," Libby said through gritted teeth.

"Uh, Libby." Georgia's voice was clipped.

Libby looked up from the ignition and followed Georgia's gaze through the passenger window.

The two black-eyed kids stood about ten paces from the car.

"Is that…"

"Shit. That's them." Libby twisted the key again, her hand trembling.

"They just teleported or something. What the hell?"

When Libby looked again, the two kids were closer, half the distance they were before.

Georgia gripped Libby's arm. "Go!"

"I'm trying."

The battery finally took and the car fired up.

Georgia shrieked again. The older kid was now right outside Georgia's window, peering in with his pure-black eyes. Through Libby's window was the younger one who'd scratched her. He smiled in at her, seemingly amused by their fear.

Libby threw the car into drive and stomped on the gas pedal. The BMW took off, jolting both her and Georgia. Libby jerked the steering wheel to the left and spun to make a U-turn while the tires squealed on the pavement.

Libby sped toward the garage exit, thankful that the barrier wasn't down. She blew over the speed bump, bottoming out Bill's BMW with a rough grinding sound. Both Libby and Georgia bounced in their seats since neither of them had had a chance to put their seatbelts on.

"Ugh, that was so freaky," Georgia said.

Libby glanced into the rearview mirror. The two boys had reappeared, standing on the edge of the parking garage entrance and watching the girls go. They faded from view as Libby put more distance between them.

"Now you've met what we've been dealing with all night," Libby said. "I told you this wasn't a game."

"They gave me such a bad feeling." Georgia put her hand over her heart just under her throat. "Right here. Like I had a giant hole in my chest."

Libby's pulse pounded as she merged onto Arnold Boulevard. It was the quickest way to get to Plaster Road. Thankfully, they were only car on the road in the early morning hours.

"They were a lot different from Karax," Georgia said. "I guess demons come in all shapes and sizes."

"You got that right. But they are equally as dangerous."

"Does that mean they know what we're planning to do?"

"For sure." Libby kept both hands on the wheel. She focused on the road ahead, hoping a cop didn't pull her over for speeding.

The painted lines on the road fell away underneath the car. Libby's breathing and pounding heart finally leveled out. All she wanted was to get back to the others. She and Georgia would be a lot safer with her dad and Miller.

"Libby…" Georgia stared into the passenger-side mirror.

Libby checked the rearview. There were sharp movements in the dark distance behind them.

The two black-eyed kids were sprinting after the car. Their legs were only a blur, like a cheetah bounding across the savannah. The streetlights extinguished one after the other as the kids passed them.

They were catching up.

29

"Hold on." Libby pushed the gas all the way to the floor. The BMW revved and picked up. Sixty miles per hour, then seventy.

"Faster!" Georgia shouted, watching the black-eyed kids get closer in the mirror.

"They're going to catch us," Libby said. She couldn't outrun them.

Libby watched in horror as the younger kid fell forward and began running on his hands and feet like an animal. He leapt into the air, momentarily vanishing from sight. A heavy thump landed on the roof of the car, denting it.

The older kid appeared beside Libby's window, keeping pace, glaring in at her.

Libby swerved at him, but the kid dodged to the side. He snarled at her in response. He leapt closer and struck the window. The glass shattered and the entire car lurched to the right from the force of his inhuman strength.

The younger kid reappeared, his head dipping upside-down from atop the car, looking in through the windshield. He pounded his fists on the glass, causing it to splinter and crack more and more with each blow.

"Seatbelt," Libby said, reaching for hers and clicking it into place. As soon as she heard Georgia do the same, Libby jammed both feet onto the brakes.

The seatbelt locked around Libby, biting into the soft skin of her throat. The kid on top hurled forward while the older kid sprinted ahead.

As the tires screeched on the road, Libby lost control of the car. It spun in circles, kicking up smoke. The world blurred in the windows, and Libby squeezed her eyes shut, praying the car wouldn't flip.

When they came to a halt, Libby hesitated before opening her eyes again. The smell of burned rubber assaulted her nostrils.

"Are you okay?" she asked Georgia. Georgia panted and gasped, trying to catch her breath through her oxygen tube.

"Where are we?" Georgia asked.

It took Libby a few moments to understand what Georgia was asking. "What the hell?"

They were off-road somewhere, parked in the grass. There was a smattering of trees around them.

Libby twisted in her seat and scanned the area, looking for Arnold Boulevard. Had they spun off the street entirely? That wasn't possible. Everything had happened very quickly, yes, but where they were now looked entirely different from where they had been.

Libby opened the door, but Georgia reached over and gripped her arm.

"Where are you going?"

"To figure out where we are and how to get back to the road."

"What if they're still out there?"

"They probably are," Libby said. "That means we have to find the way back even faster."

Libby climbed out of the car and surveyed her environment. Arnold Boulevard was nowhere in sight.

Georgia got out, reinserting her nasal cannula. "I don't get it. Where the hell are we?"

"It's them," Libby said. "They're doing this to us." It was the only reasonable explanation.

Scratches completely marked up the sides of Bill's BMW. Some were small, while others reached all along the side of the car. All were in sets of three.

There was movement above. Something rustled in the tree branches overhead. It sounded like a squirrel jumping from one limb to the other.

A terrible feeling came over Libby. Georgia rushed to Libby's side and linked arms with her, and the two girls stood together as the sounds continued.

"You were right. Let's get back in the car," Libby said.

But as soon as she turned, they were there. The black-eyed kids leaned from behind a thick tree trunk, one on each side, peeking around at them as if playing a game of hide and seek.

"Go away. Leave us alone," Libby demanded.

The two kids popped back behind the trunk, hidden from view again.

Georgia leaned into the BMW through the driver's side and emerged with the cross she'd taken from the chapel. She clutched it close to her chest.

She pointed. "There."

Libby turned. The kids had reappeared. They sprinted directly toward the girls.

The kids jumped into the air in unison, springing high, arcing toward them with hands outstretched, ready to grab. Their mouths were open, baring sharp teeth.

Libby turned away and shielded her face. Georgia thrust the cross between them and the pouncing demons.

Before the kids' extended hands could touch Libby and Georgia, the pair vanished in a burst of black smoke. The cloud engulfed both Libby and Georgia, blocking their vision and making them cough. It smelled strongly of sulfur.

Libby waved her hands, dissipating the smoke.

A car horn blared.

Libby and Georgia now stood in the middle of Arnold Boulevard, holding each other. The wide lanes, asphalt, and painted lines had all returned. Georgia still had the cross extended in front of them.

A honking car swerved around them.

"We're back," Georgia said.

Bill's BMW was parked nearby, both car doors open. The dents, scratches, and cracked glass still marred its once-sleek body.

"I don't get it," Georgia said.

"It was all an illusion created by the kids," Libby said. "You saved us."

Georgia looked down at the cross in her hands. "I remember your dad always saying religious icons would work."

"Come on. We need to get to him."

30

R and knew he was driving too fast for the winding Plaster Road. There were no street-lights; he could only see what was within the range of his headlights.

The clock on his center console drew his eye. It read 4:17 AM.

He took a curve a bit too fast, only letting up on the gas rather than tapping the brakes. The box-like form of his Jeep tipped precariously at the top of the curve.

"Why don't you slow down a bit, Rando?" Miller said from the backseat.

"Libby and Georgia are probably already there." Rand said flatly. At that point, he was not particularly in the mood to be told what to do. Beside him, Stacy shifted uncomfortably in the passenger seat. She stared out the window, arms folded.

Rand wondered what was tumbling through her head. Probably more of the same—blaming herself and wondering what she did wrong. Although Rand had tried to console her, he knew Stacy would only continue to feel it was her fault, at least until this whole situation could be resolved. Or maybe she would never forgive herself for what she'd put her friend Kim through.

Despite the pothole's size, Rand saw it too late. It looked like a crater on the surface of the moon. Because of his speed, Rand didn't have time to swerve. His front driver's-side tire fell into the hole with a crash, jolting his Jeep sharply to the left. Rand swore as he gripped the wheel with both hands and pressed on his brake for the first time since being on Plaster Road.

The tire underneath rumbled loose as it deflated, and the entire car leaned. Rand eased to the side of the road and stopped.

"What did you run over?" Miller asked.

Rand threw off his seatbelt and stepped out to inspect the damage. As he thought, his tire was completely flat.

He stared at it for a long time. As he did, an angry energy began to well up inside him. It seemed to sprout in the back of his head and spread slowly down his chest and take root in his heart.

Rand had seen many flat tires before, but this one was different. This *meant* something. Of all the bad luck he'd had in his life, this might have been the worst timed.

Rand surprised himself when he started chuckling, because nothing about what was happening was remotely funny. The mirth seemed to come from nowhere. Perhaps it was his body trying to combat the seething anger that was about to boil over.

He couldn't stop himself. Before he knew what was happening, he was laughing so hard that tears came to his eyes.

"Mr. Casey?"

He was aware that Stacy had gotten out of the car and was now looking at him as if he'd lost his mind. Maybe he had. Couldn't she see why this was funny?

"Rando." Miller was there too. Rand hadn't seen either of them get out of the car. "Are you all right?"

Rand thrust his hand toward the tire. "Look, Miller. We have a flat." He wiped the edges of his eyes.

"Yeah," Miller said. His tone cautious, as if he was speaking to someone who'd just escaped from an asylum. "You hit a pretty nasty pothole. Why are you laughing?"

"Can't you see?" Rand said, but when he looked at his friend, then at Stacy, he saw that neither of them were laughing along. "A *pothole*, Miller. A hole in the road has blown out my tire. At the *worst* possible time."

"Yeah, buddy," Miller said, venturing to put his hand on Rand's shoulder. Rand recoiled. In that moment, the thought of being touched repulsed him. It belittled his frustration. Miller slowly lowered his hand as if it were a weapon. "These things happen. Especially out here on Plaster Road, where they never repave the streets."

Rand felt another wave of laughter coming on. "I've had demons blow out my tires. Or knock them off completely. Sometimes all four at once. I've had phantom cars try to run me off the road." He gesticulated wildly as he made his point. "I've had apparitions appear right in front of my path, trying to get me to swerve. All of it."

"Yeah…"

"And now that we're in such a big hurry… now that timing matters more than anything… there's a *pothole*. Just a *pothole*."

He caught a glimpse of Stacy. The girl had worn a

fearful expression for most of the night, but now it was aimed at him.

"It's okay, Rando," Miller said. "We'll put the spare on, then—"

"It *isn't* okay, Miller," Rand snapped, and his friend took a step back. His laughter was gone now, disappearing as fast as it had come. "It *isn't* just a pothole. If *God* is on our side, don't you think he's powerful enough to help me miss a stupid little *pothole* right when it fucking counts?"

Miller looked confused. He ventured to speak. "I see what you mean, but—"

"No, you don't." Rand could see his friend was only placating him, trying to get him to shut up and continue on, but what was the point?

"So this is about the God thing, then."

"It's *always* been about that."

Rand knew he wasn't going to win. That was clear to him now. If God was just going to throw potholes, of all things, in his way, then how could he count on God to be there when he faced not just one, but *two* demons from hell?

And who knew when Shindael would make another surprise appearance?

Rand started walking, passing in front of the headlights and cutting the beams of light with his shadow. He needed to get away. Just for a minute. He'd been running around frantically all night without stopping and he finally needed a time out.

"Where are you going?" Miller shouted after him.

"I just need a fucking break," Rand shouted without looking back.

He strode into the woods that lined the side of Plaster Road. The thick mounds of leaves brushed up against his ankles as he plowed through them.

The farther Rand got away from his headlights, the darker it became. Soon, he couldn't see anything. His shoe caught on a thick tree root. Rand flailed his arms to keep his balance, but it was too late. Gravity took him. He fell forward onto his stomach and ate dead leaves and dirt as the air was knocked from his lungs.

He rolled onto his back and stared up into the darkness. The treetops blocked out the night sky, so he couldn't even the stars or the moon. He felt like he was in a coffin, buried alive.

Fitting. At least if he were six feet under he wouldn't be around to bring pain to everyone around him.

Ever since his last case, Rand had considered the idea that God was not with him at all. Never had been. He was alone in his fight against the demonic.

This night confirmed it.

He remembered what Tessa had said. *Maybe you should move very far away from us.*

Fine. He didn't need any more convincing. As soon as the sun came up, he'd pack a bag and be on his way. It was in everyone's best interest. He saw that now, thanks to a pothole.

Rand thought about how huge that hole had been. Maybe it had taken years to grow to that size. He imagined God sitting on his throne, watching that hole in the street get wider and deeper with every tire that ran over it, knowing it was being cultivated for this very moment.

He heard something between the trees.

Rand rolled over onto his stomach and looked deeper

into the woods. A bright light had appeared in the distance between the thick tree trunks, white and shimmering.

Rand clenched his eyes shut and opened them again. The light was still there. Coming closer, even. As if floating toward him.

Now I'm seeing things, he thought.

As the light neared, his muscles relaxed. The tension eased from his limbs. His heart rate slowed. The over-powering negative thoughts left him as if chased away.

Am I dying?

There was certainly a white light. He had guided lost spirits toward the white light a countless number of times. Was this the same white light?

It felt so good. It had to be death.

But why am I dying? Did I hit my head when I fell?

The light was closer now. It was too radiant to look at directly, and Rand had to squint.

Somewhere in the back of his mind, he knew he couldn't die. Not now. If he did, who would help Stacy? Who would save Kim?

"Mr. Casey?"

The sound of his name came from behind him. He twisted where he lay on the ground and followed the voice. He was met by an even brighter light, but one far less comforting. A flashlight from a cell phone.

Stacy wielded it as approached. "Mr. Casey, what are you doing on the ground?"

Rand pushed himself to a sitting position and looked behind him again. The white light was gone, and now there was only darkness.

"Did you see that?" Rand asked.

"See what?"

He pointed. "There was a—" He paused. He didn't know *what* it had been.

"Mr. Casey, you're scaring me."

Rand looked back to Stacy, his hallucinations forgotten. What she'd just said dropped him back into reality like a ten-ton stone. Of all the things that she'd experienced tonight, *he* was the one scaring her?

He climbed to his feet and brushed off the leaves that clung to his jacket. Smudges of dirt remained on his jeans and his palms. "I…"

Stacy slung her arms around his torso and buried her cheek into his chest, pulling him into a tight hug. Rand was dumbfounded, wondering what he'd done to deserve that. Nothing. She was just comforting him the only way she knew how.

"You're at your breaking point," Stacy said, her voice shaking. "You've been doing so much for me all night and it isn't fair." She looked up at him now. "Go home, Mr. Casey. I'll go meet Georgia at the lot and find Kim."

Rand wondered where this was coming from. "What do you mean? You can't go alone."

"And you can't keep on like this," Stacy said, taking a step away from him. "I'm sorry I asked you to do all this for me. You've already done so much, but this is my problem. Not yours. I can take it from here."

Rand could hear how hard Stacy was trying to sound strong. Despite her valiant words, she still looked stricken with fear. Despite that, Rand realized she was resolved to take the matter into her own hands.

"Stacy, no. I'm not going to leave you."

"But—"

"I lost it for a minute." He still wasn't quite over that pothole. "I'm sorry you had to see that. But I'm here for you until the end."

"Are you sure?"

"Yes. Come on," Rand said.

They walked together out of the woods and back to Plaster Road while Stacy used the phone flashlight to illuminate their way. Rand spotted the gnarled root that had brought him down.

When they got back to the road, Rand saw Miller leaning against the Jeep, holding the jack that Rand kept in his trunk. "You good, Rando?"

"Yeah," Rand said. "I just needed a minute." He wiped at his face and ran his hand through his hair. "Let's get this spare on."

Miller thrust the jack into Rand's chest, the metal tool stabbing into his sternum. "Already done."

"You changed the tire?"

Miller gave him an incredulous look. "You haven't figured out how this works yet? We're a team, Rando. You fight the demons while I hide away scared. You ask questions about a case while I find the answers. You have a breakdown in the forest while I change the tire. Got it? Now can we get moving?"

31

L ibby steered the car into the empty lot on Plaster Road. The uneven terrain caused the BMW—not being designed for off roading—to rock and bounce.

When the headlights cut through the darkness, she did not see her dad's orange Jeep.

She'd figured her dad would have arrived already, given their little detour on the Arnold Road Extension.

"Hmm… I hope nothing's happened," Libby said, pulling her cell phone from her pocket. Then Georgia's breathing turned into sharp, rapid gasps. "What's wrong? Are you out of oxygen in your tank?"

Georgia shook her head. She looked petrified. "It's this lot. There's…"

"Do you sense something? Already?"

Georgia looked at her. "What happened here? I've never felt anything like this. This is *way* worse than anything at the hospital." Georgia threw open her car door and climbed out.

"Hey, where are you going?" Libby said, following the other girl. "Maybe we should wait for my dad."

Georgia walked deeper into the empty lot, pulling her oxygen tank on wheels behind her. The headlights from the BMW cast Georgia's long shadow onto the dead grass.

Libby didn't follow her friend. She'd seen enough mediums to know that once they got going, it was best to leave them alone and not interrupt.

Georgia paused in the center of the lot. She looked from side-to-side, up and down. Then she turned right and walked deliberately, as if following a faint trail. She stopped and pivoted on her heel, as if whatever she was tracking had suddenly changed directions. She followed the new path for a bit before halting again. She twisted her head in each direction, as if trying to pay attention to many things at once.

Libby folded her arms and shivered as she watched the other girl. The workings of the spiritual realm never ceased to amaze Libby. Georgia looked like she was playing a game of tag with a bunch of imaginary friends.

Even though Georgia was many paces away from Libby, she heard sobbing. Something had upset Georgia.

Libby started walking farther onto the lot. When Georgia heard her coming, she paused.

"Something horrible happened here," Georgia said, wiping her eyes.

"What did you see?" Libby asked.

"I don't really know. There's a bunch of spirits here. They all feel different, and they're all moving."

"Moving?"

"Yeah."

"What are they doing?" Libby asked.

"I don't know. I can't see those details." She paused. "But I can feel. There's *so* much negative energy in this place."

"You should stop." Libby was sterner with her suggestion this time. "We shouldn't mess around with this until my dad gets here. He can help you figure out what you're sensing."

"But there's one that's not like the others." Georgia took several long, deliberate paces to the side and planted herself in a certain spot. "She's right here. All the others are moving around the lot, but this one hasn't left this place the whole time."

Libby shrugged. "I don't know what that means. Again, my dad—"

"I can't communicate with it," Georgia said. "I tried and no one's answering me. But I can just barely see…"

Georgia closed her eyes. She hesitated like that for several long moments. Her brow furrowed. "Hmm... That can't be right."

"What do you see?"

Georgia's eyes sprang open and she looked confused. "That's weird."

"What is it?"

"I saw—"

Another car pulled onto the lot. The orange Jeep's headlights pierced through the darkness.

"Oh, good," Libby said. "Come on. You can tell my dad everything you just told me."

32

Bill's BMW was already there when Rand pulled into the empty lot. He parked next to the car. He immediately noticed the long scratches gouged into the car's black paint. The BMW had been beaten to hell and back.

"What the hell?"

He leapt from the car seat and took a closer look. The windshield was cracked, the top of the roof had a huge dent, and there were more scratches on the other side of the car.

"Dad." His daughter approached him from the other side of the lot. Georgia Collins was behind her, oxygen tank trailing.

"Libby, are you two okay?"

"Yes, we're fine."

"What happened to Bill's car?"

"The black-eyed kids came after us. We got away, though."

Miller and Stacy came around, both eyeing the car.

"Good to see you again, Ghost Man," Georgia said.

"You too. Sorry to ruin your Halloween."

"Hey, man. I owe you big time. So anything you need, I'm here to help you out."

I wish she wasn't so enthusiastic about this, Rand thought. "Why didn't you tell me as soon as you started having clairvoyant visions?" His tone was scolding.

"I was going to," Georgia said, rolling her eyes. "But Libby told me to wait until after Halloween, because you apparently turn into a psycho."

Rand glared at Libby. She shrugged. "Right. We'll hash this out later. For now, we need to get to work." He started walking deep into the lot, but Georgia grabbed his arm and stopped him.

"I've already sensed things."

Rand looked down at her. "Really?"

"The spiritual activity here is really strong. I felt it as soon as we got here."

"What did you see?"

"There are lots of presences here. They're moving around all over the place. I don't know what they're doing, but there's a lot of negativity."

"No surprise there," Miller chimed in.

"Tell him what you told me," Libby said. "About there being one that's different."

"Oh yeah. One of them isn't like the rest. It's standing still while all the others are moving around the area."

To Rand, that was a step in the right direction. Whenever groups of spirits were present, it was usually helpful to focus on the one that was most different from the others. The outlier was usually able to give the best information.

He was quite impressed with how much Georgia was able to discern without having had much practice.

"Do you know anything about this one that's standing still?" Rand asked. "Were you able to communicate, or…"

"I saw something, but it doesn't make sense," Georgia said, looking at the ground. "I'm new at this, remember? It's probably a mistake."

"What did you see?"

Georgia looked up at him and hesitated. "A black cat." She shrugged. "I don't know what it means. Maybe a symbol. Maybe nothing. I do like cats, so maybe I was just trying to think of something to make me feel better from all the—"

"That's Kim!" Stacy said.

Rand and the others turned. All eyes were on Stacy now. "What?"

"Kim was going to be a black cat for Halloween," Stacy explained. "She was getting ready for the Boyd Street party when I was on the phone with her. She would have been wearing her costume when she got taken."

Rand turned back to Georgia. "A black cat. You're sure?"

"Yes.Wait, you mean I'm not wrong?"

"Where did you sense the black cat?"

Georgia led the way to a point near the back of the lot. Rand and all the others followed her. She stopped in a very precise location, as if she had followed a treasure map to a spot marked with an X.

"Here."

Rand looked around. So did the others.

"So Kim is here," Stacy said, "but also not here?"

"The black-eyed kids brought her," Rand said. "But we can't see her."

"She's invisible or something?" Stacy asked.

"She's standing right where I am," Georgia said. "I can feel it. And I can see the black cat again. It's very clear."

"What does it mean, Miller?" Rand asked.

"Maybe she was taken to the spiritual dimension," Miller said. "It's possible to be alive and visit there."

"How do we get her back?" Stacy asked.

"It has to do with time," Libby said.

Everyone looked at her.

"Time for what?" Miller asked.

Libby ignored him. "Dad, when was the Arnold Road Extension built?"

"I don't know," Rand said, wondering what his daughter was thinking. "Why?"

"Arnold Road's been there forever," Miller said.

"Not Arnold Road," Libby said. "The *extension*. That new part. When was that built?"

"Oh. Umm..." Miller scratched at his stubbled chin. "I don't know. A few decades ago. But the road itself was—"

"When the black-eyed kids attacked us on the extension, our car spun out and we suddenly weren't on the road anymore. The whole thing had disappeared."

"Oh yeah," Georgia said. "That was weird."

"And then when Georgia chased them away with the cross, the road reappeared."

It took Rand a few moments to piece together what Libby was telling him. "Time distortion."

"What?" Libby asked.

"When the black-eyed kids were in my car, I passed a Gavin's Deli."

"Impossible," Miller said. "They went out of business years ago. Which is a shame because their roast beef melt—"

"I knew that was strange, but I didn't make the connection earlier. I was seeing the past."

"And when I saw the black-eyed kids at the party," Libby added, "everyone around me looked like they were from the eighties. I thought it was a bunch of Halloween costumes, but…"

"That's it," Rand said, a surge of energy coursing through him. "The black-eyed kids are anchored to the Erlich family murders from 1984. When we're near them, sometimes we see what the world looked like at that time." Rand looked at Stacy. "And Stacy, you lost two hours the first time the black-eyed kids came to your door, right?" Stacy nodded.

Rand was almost embarrassed he'd missed it. It made so much sense. Time distortion was a common side effect of being near a demonic entity. Usually it seemed more like a slowing or a quickening of the present time, but every so often, one could glimpse the past. Other times, the future.

"So Kim is trapped in the past?" Stacy asked. She still looked confused.

"The black-eyed kids brought her there," Rand said. "Those other spirits that Georgia senses must be the Erlich family. The one that feels different is Kim."

"She's still right here," Georgia said, pointing at her feet. "But you're saying she's in this spot as it existed thirty years go, right?"

"Yes," Rand said.

"So, how do we get into the past?"

Rand knew the answer. Judging by the silence that descended on the group, he figured everyone else had arrived at the same conclusion.

The past could be accessed when the black-eyed kids were near. That meant he needed them to come.

"Mr. Casey..." Stacy peered toward the cars. She pointed a trembling finger.

Two black figures stood in the beams of the Jeep's headlights, swallowing the light.

33

"Get behind me," Rand said as he stepped forward. The others obeyed.

Both the Jeep and BMW still had their headlights on. The four bright beams were broken only by the black forms of the two kids, standing side-by-side. None of their features were visible.

"Georgia," Libby whispered behind Rand. "Where's the cross?"

"I left it in the car."

Rand took another step forward. "Hey! I'm here. I'm who you came for, right? So go ahead."

"Dad," Libby said.

"Mr. Casey, what are you doing?"

Neither of the black-eyed kids moved. They stood still like mannequins.

"What are you afraid of?" Rand shouted.

The two shadows took a step forward in unison. As soon as they did, all four headlights shut off. The entire lot was plunged into total darkness.

Rand could no longer see them. He heard frantic shuffling behind him. One cell phone light turned on, followed by another. Then a third. Those beams swept the area, but it was very hard to see anything. They weren't powerful enough for the expansive lot.

Rand heard footsteps to his left. Then whispers to his right. Then rustling in the trees overhead.

"Stop playing games," he called into the darkness. He spread his arms wide. "I'm here. Come and take me."

Leaves rustled somewhere in front of him. The others must have heard it too, because all three cell phone lights turned in that direction at the same time.

The beams lit up one of the black-eyed kids—the younger one—as he sprinted toward Rand.

He leapt forward like some kind of animal, then opened his mouth and bared his teeth.

Libby cried out. Stacy screamed.

Rand's instincts told him to shield himself or dodge, but he resisted. Instead, he waited for the child to make contact so he could be taken to the past.

The force of the demon struck him in the chest like a battering ram. Rand was knocked off his feet. Before he even hit the ground, his entire world went black.

34

Stacy had only seen the younger black-eyed kid at the last second.

He'd soared through the air, arms outstretched, illuminated only by the meager beam of her cell phone. She'd been knocked off her feet. She remembered pain that disappeared just as quickly as it had come. Her vision had darkened and her mind had quieted, and Stacy wondered if that was what it felt like to die.

But she was awake now, lying flat on her back.

As clarity returned, Stacy used her elbows to force herself to a seated position. The effort it took to sit up was astounding, leaving her fatigued.

"What happened?" Speaking took more strength than sitting.

Stacy's eyes adjusted. She looked around. She was alone.

Mr. Casey was gone. So was his friend Miller, and his daughter. Georgia as well.

"Mr. Casey?" Panic crept in. "Mr. Casey?"

Stacy looked behind her. Everything had changed. The empty lot was no longer just a barren patch of land. A house had appeared. It was simple, small, and plain. Children's toys were scattered in the yard and the grass was overgrown. There were no lights on inside.

"Mr. Casey?" Stacy whispered again, her voice trembling.

"Stacy." Mr. Casey's voice was loud behind her, and it startled her. She twisted around in the grass, relieved that her teacher had found her.

But it was Georgia who was standing behind her. But there was something strange about her. Georgia was alone, back straight and hands by her side. Her eyes were closed, as if she was sleeping. And although it was suddenly very windy, her clothes or hair were not blowing.

"Stacy, can you hear me?"

It sounded like Mr. Casey's voice was coming from Georgia. Georgia's mouth did not move.

"Yes, I'm here." Stacy said. "Where are you?"

"I'm communicating with you through Georgia," Mr. Casey said.

It took Stacy a few moments to make sense of it all. She was in the past, and the others were still in the present. Georgia, with her sensitive abilities, was able to communicate with the past from the present. Stacy figured this was what it felt like to be a ghost speaking to a medium that was reaching out to the spiritual world during a séance.

"Listen to me, Stacy," Mr. Casey said. "They took you."

"I know. I can see the past. The Erlich house is here."

After a few seconds of silence, Mr. Casey said, "We can get you out of there."

"How?"

Georgia moved for the first time since she'd appeared. She extended her hand straight ahead of her, palm stretched toward the sky. Her eyes remained closed, trance-like.

"Can you see Georgia?" Mr. Casey asked.

"Yeah. She's right in front of me."

"Good. Take her hand," Mr. Casey said. "She is a bridge between the two time periods. If you take her hand, you'll come back to the present."

"What? How?"

"Your body and soul belong here, so when they are displaced, like they are right now, they will always look for a way back. Connecting with your true world will return you to where you belong. Take Georgia's hand. You'll see."

Stacy pushed herself to a standing position. Georgia remained still, hand outstretched, offering her a way back to the present.

Could it really be that simple? Stacy wondered. Mr. Casey sounded very certain. He'd probably experienced this situation before in one of his cases.

"Mr. Casey, Kim is inside the house," Stacy said.

"I know. But so are the black-eyed kids. That house is where they are anchored, remember? As soon as you come back, then I can find a way to access the past."

Stacy did remember, and she felt ill being reminded. It was like being in enemy territory. Here, in this illusion that surrounded her, the black-eyed kids were in charge. But still, she hesitated to take Georgia's hand.

"Stacy?" Mr. Casey asked. "What are you waiting for?"

"I'm sorry, but I can't." The words tumbled out, surprising even her.

"What do you mean? It's simple. Just touch Georgia."

"It's isn't that. It's just…"

"Stacy." Mr. Casey's voice was stern. A warning. He probably knew what she was thinking.

It wasn't fair. Kim being taken was Stacy's fault. Mr. Casey running all over town trying to help Kim was *also* Stacy's fault. Libby and her mother had also seen the black-eyed kids. Georgia was now involved. Stacy deserved all the blame. She remembered how broken Mr. Casey had become on the side of Plaster Road. The events of the night had pushed him to the edge. She simply wouldn't be able to live with herself if something happened to him.

"I'm going inside the house to get Kim," Stacy announced.

"You can't do that," Mr. Casey said. "It's too dangerous. You need to come back and let me go instead."

"I was the one they wanted in the first place," Stacy said. "This is where they meant to bring me. Well, I'm here now. I can fix this."

"Stacy." Mr. Casey's voice was steady, trying to reason with her. "You won't just walk inside that house and get Kim. It won't be that simple. There is *always* a trick."

"I know. I take your class, remember?"

"Stacy. Don't do this. Please."

"I'm sorry, Mr. Casey. I'll come back, I promise. And when I do, Kim will be with me."

She turned away from Georgia and started walking toward the house.

Mr. Casey's protests grew quieter as Stacy got farther away from Georgia, until they were just a noise in the distance. Soon, Stacy couldn't hear him at all.

Then came the first sign of movement from the house. Someone jogged from around the back, along the side, and toward Stacy. She froze where she stood.

It was the younger black-eyed kid. His bare feet pattered on the grass. He still wore his grimy black t-shirt and shorts.

He stopped a few feet from her and looked up at her with his pure-black eyes. Then, smiling, he lifted his hand and pointed at the house.

35

S tacy walked toward the house. When she reached the front porch, she turned around, but the child had vanished. Georgia remained in the distance, her hand outstretched, waiting for Stacy to return.

The black-eyed kids were here. At least, the younger one was. They were watching her. What would they do when she got close to Kim?

When Stacy approached the front door, it opened by itself, as if the house was pleased to welcome her into a nightmare. Stacy took a steadying breath. She was just about to step inside when she heard a car behind her.

A pickup trunk barreled off the road and into the yard, zipping narrowly past where Georgia still stood. It ran over a yellow toy car before it ground to a stop.

The door flew open and a round, stocky guy spilled out. He was haggard, with disheveled black hair and sweat stains on his white t-shirt. The man upended a bottle of whiskey into his mouth and drained what remained, then tossed the empty bottle to the other side of the yard. He reached into the bed of his truck and pulled out a shotgun.

He marched forward, directly toward Stacy. Fear seized her entire body, but the man seemed to not see her.

The armed, drunken man brushed past Stacy and went inside, not acknowledging her at all. He turned right and disappeared into the darkened house.

"Carl?" a man's voice called out. "Why do you have that gun?"

A gunshot rang out from within. A woman screamed. She was silenced by another shot. Stacy recoiled after each blast.

Stacy understood what she was seeing. She'd learned in Mr. Casey's class that spirits would sometimes play out the tragic circumstances of their deaths over and over again. Mr. Casey had told them he'd experienced it many times before, and he'd learned that oftentimes the best way to learn what kept the spirits trapped on Earth was to follow the events.

Stacy steeled herself, then went the same way the gunman had gone toward the back the house. She walked through a simple kitchen, then behind it, a hallway. The door to the first bedroom was open.

Stacy glanced inside for only a millisecond before tearing her eyes away.

A man sprawled out on the floor. A woman crumpled in the corner. Dark red had been spattered on the wall.

Stacy backed away, hand over her mouth to keep herself from vomiting as tears leaked from her eyes.

Stay strong, she thought. *I have to stay strong for Kim.*

"Bonnie," Carl barked from somewhere else in the house.

The parents, their daughter, and her two kids, Stacy remembered. *Those were the victims.*

She'd just seen the parents in the bedroom. Bonnie must be the daughter—Carl's girlfriend.

Every part of Stacy wanted to stop Carl from continuing on his rampage, but she knew it was futile.

She'd asked that very question in class when Mr. Casey had spoken of this phenomenon. He'd told her it was indeed tempting to want to alter the course of these tragic events, but it was impossible. They had already happened. Even though they still replayed over and over, there was nothing that could be done to change the past. The tragedy replaying itself on loop was what kept the negative energy in a location long after the events had happened. That negative energy attracted the demons that fed off of it.

"Where are you, Bonnie?" Carl roared, drunk and angry.

Stacy realized that someone was behind her—a young girl, perhaps only a few years older than Stacy. On either side of her were two kids, her arms protectively around their shoulders. They had shaggy hair, old clothes, and bare feet.

They looked identical to the black-eyed kids, though their wide, fearful eyes were not black. The girl crouched down and whispered something to them.

The girl hurried her sons into the hallway and past Stacy, none of them aware of her presence. The girl reached up and pulled open the hallway attic door. She unfolded the ladder and ushered her two kids up. She closed them up in their hiding place.

"Bonnie!"

The girl looked both directions down the hall, trying to decide which way to go. From what Stacy could tell, the house was one story, but large. The rooms all seemed connected, and every path led back on itself. It was a deadly labyrinth, and Stacy already knew that Bonnie would lose the game.

"Bonnie," Stacy said. Her voice echoed unnaturally, reverberating back at her, reminding her that she didn't belong there. She was an intruder in their place in time.

Stacy wasn't sure, but she thought Bonnie spared her the smallest of glances before darting forward and disappearing through a door at the end of the hallway.

Did she hear me? Stacy thought.

Stacy followed. Bonnie had retreated into what looked like the living room. She tip-toed around a large sofa, quietly advancing toward the foyer and front door, where Stacy had entered—the only escape.

But Carl appeared around the corner, his shotgun aimed at her chest. Bonnie lifted her palms and backed away from Carl, but he only pressed forward.

"Carl, what are you doing?" Bonnie said through her sobs.

"Where are the kids?" Carl's speech slurred.

"Please leave us alone," she pleaded.

Carl struck Bonnie on the chin with the butt of his shotgun and pointed it at her again.

Bonnie did not wipe the blood from her lip.

"Where are they, Bonnie?" Carl screamed at her, shaking the gun in his drunken rage.

Stacy couldn't stop herself. "Put the gun down." Although she put as much energy behind her command as she could, it still came out muted and distant.

But Stacy's voice seemed to catch Bonnie's attention. As if she could barely hear Stacy.

She can *hear me,* Stacy realized. *Even if we are in different dimensions.*

Mr. Casey had said it was impossible to change the past, but Stacy couldn't just stand by and watch Carl murder this poor girl.

"Put down the gun," Stacy yelled again.

Bonnie turned to look at Stacy. Their eyes met, and Bonnie seemed to have a moment of clarity.

"Who's there?" Bonnie whispered.

"What are you looking at?" Carl demanded.

"I'm looking for my friend," Stacy said. "My friend is here somewhere."

Bonnie's brow furrowed. "A girl?"

"Who are you talking to?" Carl spat. "Tell me where the kids are."

"Yes!" Stacy said. "Where is she?"

Carl cocked his shotgun. "Answer me!"

"In the attic," Bonnie finally whispered.

Carl smirked. Stacy knew the response was for her, but Carl thought it was for him.

Stacy looked away just in time as the blast went off. Bonnie collapsed, her body falling limp to the floor.

Stacy began to weep. What had she been thinking? Maybe Mr. Casey was right. Maybe she *should* have let him handle this. She didn't have the stomach for all this violence.

Carl stepped over Bonnie's body and went into the hallway. He eyed the attic door.

But then he turned and went the other direction, placing his gun over his shoulder. He went to the kitchen and opened a cabinet above the sink, which was filled with liquor.

"Your old man always said I was a drunk," Carl muttered to himself. "Well, takes one to know one. He won't be saying that again."

While Carl was distracted by his whiskey, Stacy took the chance to rush to the hallway, lower the attic door, and unfold the ladder.

Stacy climbed up. The attic was filled with boxes and old furniture, clutter from a family that had lived in the house for a long time. There was a path through the middle of the junk that led to the back of the attic.

The two young boys were huddled together in the corner, the older one's arms wrapped around the younger. They trembled as they watched the door.

"I'm not here to hurt you," Stacy whispered to them. They did not respond.

They can't see me.

"Who's there?" a voice called out. It was raspy and weak, as if on the verge of giving out. But it was familiar.

Stacy rushed over and around the boxes.

36

R and had never felt so helpless.

He paced the same small stretch of the lot over and over, waiting and worrying. Every few seconds he glanced at Georgia. She stood still, eyes closed as if she was in a trance, arm outstretched toward nothing.

Rand checked his watch. It was 5:09 in the morning.

"All that pacing is making me nervous," Miller said.

"You *should* be nervous," Rand said. "Stacy has no idea what she'll encounter where she is. I don't even know."

"She'll be okay, Dad," Libby offered. But her words sounded hollow.

"Stacy's your star student, right?" Miller said. "You've taught her well."

"It's not the same," Rand said. "You know it isn't." Sitting through his lectures was one thing. Coming face-to-face with the demonic was something else entirely.

Footsteps crunched the dry leaves somewhere in the darkness. A flashlight beam danced on the ground as someone approached. "Who's there?" Rand called, halting his pacing and standing alert.

Wayne Swanson shone the light onto his own face. He had his shotgun in the other hand.

"We're almost done here, Mr. Swanson," Rand said.

"Somethin' ain't right," Wayne said.

"I know," Rand said. "We're working on it." He glanced again at Georgia. To Wayne, she probably looked insane.

"It ain't that," Wayne said. "You've gone and done somethin' else."

Rand could see that Wayne wasn't just annoyed—he was afraid. "What's wrong?"

"You tell me. What have you stirred up 'round here?"

Rand exchanged a glance with Miller, then looked back to Wayne. "Has something happened?"

"My wife's scared out her wits, that's what's happened," he said. "And I gotta be honest, I never seen anythin' quite like that before."

"What did you see?"

"Exactly what you said I would. You told me if anyone knocks at the door, don't let them in."

Rand sighed and shook his head. "Tell me what happened. I can help you."

"You don't need to tell me," Wayne said. "You need to tell my wife. She's the one losin' it right now."

"Sure. Is she inside?"

Wayne hesitated and appraised Rand for a few seconds, probably debating whether or not to let him into the house. "Come with me." Wayne turned and started walking toward his house, shotgun resting over his shoulder, resembling like a soldier.

"You two stay here and keep an eye on Georgia," Rand

instructed. "If Stacy comes back, or anything happens, come and get me."

Miller nodded. Libby chewed her lip nervously.

Rand followed Wayne, wondering what the black-eyed kids had done this time.

37

Kim still wore the leotard and leggings of her black cat Halloween costume. A metal cuff was around her right ankle, attached to a short chain bolted to the wooden attic floor.

"Stacy!"

Stacy ran over to her friend and wrapped her in a tight hug. Kim squeezed her back.

"What's going on?" Kim said, sobbing into Stacy's neck. "What is this place?"

"I'll explain everything, but first let's get out of here."

Kim's black hair was disheveled and tangled. Her skin was milky pale. Her black makeup was streaked from her tears.

"Why am I here Stacy?" Kim's voice shook. "I don't want to be here anymore."

Stacy touched her friend's wet cheeks with both her hands. Her skin was like ice. "You don't have to be. I'm bringing you out."

"I don't want to see it anymore."

"See what?"

Kim only stared back at her through wide, bloodshot eyes.

Escape first, talk later, Stacy thought.

Stacy knelt and investigated the clamp around Kim's ankle and where the chain was fastened to the floorboard. She gave it a few yanks and the wood bent a bit.

"The floor is weak," Stacy said. "Maybe if we both pull on it—"

Kim wasn't listening. Her eyes were on the two frightened boys in the opposite corner of the attic. They were oblivious to what was happening.

"Please save them," Kim whispered.

It struck Stacy why Kim was traumatized.

The spirits of the Erlich family were reliving their tragedy on a repeating loop, Stacy thought. *Kim has watched these boys get murdered over and over again.*

Stacy was sickened at what those demons had done to Kim. They'd trapped her right where she'd be forced to repeatedly witness one of the most horrific things imaginable.

"Listen to me." Stacy snapped her fingers in front of Kim's face, commanding her focus. "This isn't real. None of this real."

"But—"

"If you don't want to see it happen again, then we need to get out of here. But we can't get out of here unless you help me. Do you understand?"

Kim's lip quivered. She nodded.

"Good. Grab this chain and help me pull it up."

Stacy and Kim both gripped the metal chain. "One.

Two. Three." They pulled together and the floorboard bent farther than the first time.

"Keep going," Stacy said through clenched teeth.

The wood cracked, then gave way. The girls stumbled as the chain ripped free.

"Follow me."

Before they could flee, however, footsteps came from the other side of the attic—heavy boots on the wooden floor. The boys started whimpering.

"Please don't," said the elder boy.

"It's happening again," Kim whispered.

Stacy set her jaw. She grabbed Kim's face and buried it into her shoulder. She clenched her own eyes shut. The shotgun went off, and the noise was deafening in the tight confines of the attic.

Kim tensed in Stacy's arms. Stacy held her friend tighter.

The gun fired again.

A few seconds after that, there was a third shot, followed by a heavy thud. The attic fell silent except for the ringing in Stacy's ears.

"Come on," Stacy whispered to Kim. "Don't look in the corner."

The two of them went for the door. Stacy refused to glance at the small bodies. What she couldn't miss, though, was Carl, sprawled out in the middle of the attic like a starfish, his shotgun lying beside him. Blood pooled around what was left of his head. Stacy and Kim stepped over him and climbed down the wooden ladder, returning to the main section of the house.

After they got down, Kim could no longer hold it

together and started sobbing. "Why does that keep happening? It never stops."

Stacy half dragged Kim along as they entered the living room. Bonnie's body should have been on the floor, but it had vanished.

The front door was still open from when she'd entered the house earlier.

"Come on," Stacy said, taking Kim by the hand. "We're almost there. I'll explain everything when—"

The door slammed shut by itself.

"Oh no."

Stacy twisted the doorknob, but it would not budge. It was as if someone were holding it closed from the other side.

"Um…. Stacy."

Something had caught Kim's attention behind them. Stacy followed her friend's gaze.

The younger black-eyed kid had appeared.

38

W ayne Swanson's front door creaked as he opened it. Rand followed the older man. The sudden warmth inside the home wrapped around Rand like a blanket. Wayne's dog, Boss, who'd been laying on his bed in the corner, rose when Rand entered.

The living room was lit only by a single reading lamp that cast a dim, eerie glow. An elderly woman stood from where she sat on the sofa. She wore a white nightgown and her silver hair was disheveled from sleep.

"This is my wife, Geraldine," Wayne said.

"You must be freezing." Geraldine seemed frazzled. "It's so cold outside tonight. I'll make you some coffee. Black, or with milk and sugar?"

"Cool it, Gerry," Wayne said. "The paranormal nut ain't got time for coffee. He's only here so we can tell him what we seen."

Rand could live with being the paranormal nut, as

long as these two were okay. "Mrs. Swanson, I understand you had some visitors earlier this evening."

Geraldine gestured to the old sofa, and Rand sat. She lowered herself onto the cushion next to him while Wayne stood nearby. He still clutched his gun.

"They knocked on the door," Geraldine began. "I was wary, because we rarely get guests, and we never have them late at night."

"They came only a few minutes after me and you spoke," Wayne interjected, "so I figured you'd followed me to ask me somethin' else."

"Who was at your door?" Rand asked, although he already knew the answer.

"The neighbor boys."

Wayne groaned. "This is what I've been tryin' to tell her," he said to Rand. "They ain't the neighbor boys. They've been dead for years, God rest their souls."

Geraldine dabbed the corner of her eye with a crumpled tissue.

When Rand had learned that the Erlich family had two boys that had died in the shooting, it made sense that the black-eyed kids were mimicking their appearance.

"I believe you, Geraldine," Rand said. "But even though those two boys looked like the ones you knew, they aren't."

"They were the spitting image," Geraldine said. "Except..." She sniffled.

"Except what?" Rand prodded.

"Their *eyes*. They were so... dark. It wasn't natural. And the way they made me feel... There was something very wrong about them."

"You didn't let them in, did you?" Rand asked.

"Hell no!" Wayne barked. "Gerry was beggin' me to, but I slammed the door in their faces. They ain't normal, and there's no chance they're comin' into my house."

"You did the right thing. Did they leave you alone after that?"

"I opened up the door again a second later, and they'd disappeared."

Rand was glad he'd remembered to warn Wayne about the black-eyed kids earlier. Otherwise, he might have let them in, especially if Geraldine thought she knew them.

"So what do we do?" Wayne asked. "I don't know much about all this, and I can't say I really believe it. But we had no issues before you showed up. Now we have a problem, and I expect you to fix it."

"I will," Rand said.

"Seems to me all you're doin' is standin' around in the lot next door shiverin' your tail off."

"I know what it looks like, but trust me, everything is under—"

Three knocks sounded on the door.

Geraldine gasped. Wayne readied his gun. Boss stiffened, ears back, a low growl rumbling from his throat.

"They're back," Geraldine whispered.

Rand rose from the couch. He stepped toward the front door.

"What do you think you're doin?" Wayne said in a harsh whisper. Geraldine went to her husband's side and linked her arm through his.

"I'll handle everything," Rand said. "Don't do anything rash."

Rand opened the door.

The older black-eyed kid stood on the porch, alone. He glared at Rand with his dark eyes.

"Let me guess," Rand said. "You need to come inside and use my telephone."

39

S tacy gasped and grabbed her friend's arm, squeezing it.

"That's one of those kids who came to the door," Kim said. "He brought me here."

"We're leaving now," Stacy declared to the kid. "This is over." She tried to make herself sound sure and authoritative. Demons had to listen, right?

'Bring me Randolph Casey.'

The words were in Stacy's head, clear as if they had come from the boy's mouth. His words were deep and dark, unlike any normal human speech. Kim looked at her, frightfully perplexed—she'd heard it too.

'Bring me Randolph Casey, and I will let you both go.'

"Why is he talking about your teacher?" Kim whispered.

Mr. Casey would be more than happy to take their place and face off against the boy. He'd wanted to be the one to enter the house and rescue Kim, after all.

Stacy caught herself, realizing what was going on. The demon had offered a deal, and she was considering it. Suddenly, she remembered the note scribbled on the inside cover of her notebook, circled and highlighted.

Not a chance, she thought.

The blank expression on the boy's face shifted into one of irritation. Stacy knew he could see into her mind and that she had figured out his bluff. He snarled at her, quick to anger.

"I will *not* bring Mr. Casey to you. We are leaving here together, and you will let us go."

The boy began to change. His human body and features dissolved away. His arms and legs became thin, wiry appendages, culminating to three sharp claws, each half a foot long. His mouth grew wider and gaping, filled with pointed teeth. The entire black form stood several feet taller than Stacy.

As the boy transformed into his true appearance, Kim squeezed Stacy's arm so hard that it began to ache. "What do we do?"

Stacy tried the door again, but it was still stuck.

The demon lifted one of his arms, poised to attack. Stacy shoved Kim away from the door while Stacy dove in the opposite direction. The claws swiped the air where the two of them had been standing a moment before. The sharp points ripped into the door, grinding three jagged marks into the wood. Stacy remembered the bloody marks on Mr. Casey's daughter's arm.

The demon turned his attention on Stacy, appearing uninterested in Kim.

Good, Stacy thought.

Stacy backed into the dining room area, moving

farther away from the exit. The demon stalked toward her.

Stacy's back bumped against the large table, blocking her retreat. The demon lifted its hand again and swiped down with incredible speed, but Stacy leapt aside.

The claw struck the table, splintering it into a bunch of wooden pieces. The table's legs buckled and snapped off, and a nearby chair caught in the crossfire also crumbled.

Stacy lost her footing and fell. She landed hard on the floor near the destroyed table. She glanced at the remains, astounded. If he had hit her instead, there would have been nothing left of her body.

"Stacy!" Kim shrieked from somewhere. "Get up!"

Stacy had to return to her feet. She couldn't maneuver if she was on the ground. The demon was already glaring at her, ready to strike again. Stacy shuffled away into the corner, now out of places of flee.

What would Mr. Casey do? Her mind raced with his stories from class. In them, he'd always been prepared. *Bibles. Holy water. Crosses.* She had none of those things.

But when she looked again at the pile of wood that remained of the table, she got an idea.

The demon lifted his clawed hand again.

Stacy didn't hesitate. She lunged forward and grabbed one of the table legs along with a piece from the chair that had been crushed. She stood and held them together to form the sign of the cross.

Immediately, the demon recoiled from it. Stacy pressed forward with her makeshift cross. The demon cowered down, pulling his arms close to his body, repelled by the holy symbol.

Now, Stacy was the one pursuing. She pushed him to

the far side of the room, into the other corner. He glared at her, furious, waiting for her to drop the cross so he could strike again.

"I command you to let my friend and I go."

The demon growled at her in protest.

Mr. Casey had taught her that the most powerful force against a demon was his own name. By using it, she could command them more authoritatively.

But I don't know his name... Stacy thought.

Mr. Casey *had* told her that this demon served a master. Given the hierarchy of hell, it made sense to Stacy that the master's name also commanded authority. Perhaps this demon even feared his master.

"You have failed, and your master"—what was the name Mr. Casey had told her?—"*Shindael* will be very unhappy."

The demon let out a low groan.

Stacy had sent the kids away once, earlier in the night. She could do it again.

She took another step forward, still holding the cross as a barrier between her and the demon.

"There will be a terrible punishment for your failure. You should leave the real work to your superiors."

The demon snarled at her, and then began to dissipate. His body turned into black smoke that sank through the floor, sucking in through the cracks in the floorboards.

Stacy waited a few seconds after he'd vanished to make sure he was really gone, then dropped the two broken pieces of wood.

Kim had watched the whole thing from around the corner, half hidden behind the wall. "Is it gone?"

"Yes."

Her friend looked at her as if she were from another planet. "How did you know how to do all that?"

"I pay attention in class."

40

R and moved aside, and the black-eyed kid did not hesitate. He stepped inside, his bare feet pattering on the hardwood floor as he walked into the living room and around the sofa toward the back of the house. He moved as if he'd lived in the house his whole life and knew where he was going.

Wayne and Geraldine watched him with wide-eyed fear, and Boss growled at him from Wayne's side. The kid didn't acknowledge any of them as he turned the corner and walked out of sight.

"What are you doin'?" Wayne whispered. "Why'd you let him into my house? Get rid of him."

Rand went into the kitchen. The black-eyed kid sat at the head of the table, his back to Rand. Rand pulled up a chair and sat down facing the kid. The demon turned toward Rand, fixing black eyes on him again.

"Where's your friend?" Rand asked.

The black-eyed kid smirked.

'He's with the girl.'

The voice echoed in Rand's head. Telepathic communication, just like Shindael used.

Stacy, Rand thought.

His mouth went dry and dread settled in the pit of his stomach. The boy continued to smirk.

Wayne appeared at the entrance of the kitchen, still holding his gun. Rand lifted his hand toward him, though, and the man stopped where he was.

"You've finally got me here," Rand said. "What is it you want from me?"

'It doesn't work like that.'

Rand set his jaw. The demon could read his mind. See his plan. That meant Rand had to coerce him a little more.

"You don't want to miss your opportunity," Rand said. "You're just another one of Shindael's slaves."

The kid's smirk was replaced by a glare. Even his eyes seemed to grow darker than they had been before.

"What better way to gain favor with the devil than to capture me right here and now? What are you waiting for?"

Rand knew that demons were fiercely prideful. There was a clear hierarchy in hell, and the lower ones despised those who were favored by the devil.

The kid bared his teeth and leaned forward, placing his palms flat on the table. Black plasma leaked from the corners of his mouth.

"Shindael will always use you," Rand pressed, "At least until you do something meaningful, like take me. Shindael himself could not even do that. Imagine the rewards."

The black-eyed kid began to transform, and his child-like disguise melted away. He grew in height until his head almost touched the ceiling. The black plasma oozed off his body and dripped onto the floor, leaving puddles between his feet. Each of his hands were made up of three long claws.

Rand stood and backed away. The demon roared at Rand so loudly that he had to cover his ears to block out the pain in his head.

The horrible sound was cut short by a gunshot.

A hole appeared in the demon's body and rancid plasma splattered across Rand's face and clothes. Wayne stood at the kitchen's entrance, smoke drifting from the barrel of his gun.

The demon crumpled over and lost his footing, his clawed hands going to the wound in his stomach, as if surprised to be attacked from behind.

Human weapons would never be effective against a creature like this, but there was no way Wayne Swanson would know that.

Rand rushed to the other side of the kitchen and lowered Wayne's shotgun. "Come on."

He yanked Wayne back into the living room. Geraldine trembled in the corner, covering her ears with her hands, shielding them from the loud gunshots. Rand gripped her by the elbow. He hurried the elderly couple toward the front door.

Behind them, Rand heard the demon's feet stomping in pursuit. The furniture crashed as he knocked out of his path.

Rand threw open the door and the three of them burst out into the cold. Boss brushed by Rand's leg as the dog bolted from the house alongside them.

Miller was in the yard. "What the hell is going on in there? I heard a gunshot." Something behind Rand caught Miller's eye, and he froze.

Rand turned. The demon stood just on the other side of the door, but no longer chased them. He lingered there for a moment before dipping back inside the dark house. The door closed by itself.

"W-what the hell was that thing?" Wayne pointed a trembling finger toward his house.

"Are you crazy?" Rand shouted at Wayne. "Guns won't hurt them. You'll just piss them off."

"Rand," Miller said, a cautioning tone in his voice.

"What do you expect me to do?" Wayne shot back. "Just sit there? Did you see what I saw?"

"Of course. It's—"

"Rand." Miller grasped Rand's shoulder. Rand took a breath and forced himself to calm.

He reminded himself that if he'd been in Wayne's shoes, he'd probably have done the same thing. He removed his jacket and placed it on Geraldine's bare shoulders.

"I got him right in the chest and it didn't even slow him down," Wayne muttered.

Geraldine started sobbing. Wayne put his arm around his wife and she leaned into him.

"I assume that's the black-eyed kid's true form," Miller said.

"Yes. One of them's in the house, and the other is with Stacy," Rand told Miller. "Has she come back yet?"

Miller only shook his head, and Rand sighed. The longer Stacy was gone, the higher the likelihood she'd gotten hurt.

"I tried to get that one to capture me and bring me to where Stacy is, but he refused."

"Of course he did," Miller said. "He knows your plan. It isn't going to be that simple." He reached out and dabbed his fingertip into a glob of plasma that remained on Rand's jacket. He rubbed it between his fingers as he inspected it. "These guys are so disgusting."

"I need to get them to take me," Rand said.

"How?" Miller asked. "They won't do it. They want Stacy separated from you. So unless you have a time machine…"

Rand ran a hand through his hair. Miller was right.

"She's your best student, right?" Miller asked. "Do you think she knows how to handle herself?"

Rand blew out his breath and put his hands on his hips as he thought. "If anyone does, it would be her."

"Then maybe you're worrying too much," Miller said. "If you've taught her well…"

"Still. It should be me in there, not her."

"True. But it *isn't* you in there."

"So what do I do?" Rand asked, more to himself than to Miller. "I can't just stand around here waiting." He turned toward the house. "I have to go back in there."

"Are you *nuts?*" Wayne said.

"He won't leave your house until he's forcefully removed."

Wayne exchanged a worried glance with his wife.

"I may as well do what I can while we wait for Stacy to make it back," Rand muttered. All he could do was pray that the girl was okay.

"Here." Miller held out the cross that Georgia had

brought with her from the hospital. "This is the only thing we have." Rand took it. "Do you want me to come in with you?" The question came out thin and tense.

"No. Stay out here with Libby and Georgia," Rand said. He turned to Wayne. "No matter what happens, don't go back inside your house until I come out. Do you understand?"

Wayne nodded.

Rand had never been completely without fear when entering a place where a known demon was waiting and lurking. He probably never would be. But his cases always came to this. He was the one who had to fight so that the demon's victims could be freed.

When Rand went back inside the house, the living room was dark. The lamp that had lit the room earlier must have been smashed during the demon's pursuit.

The door behind him slammed shut by itself. Rand whirled, startled. He tried the knob, already knowing what he'd find. It was stuck, held closed by an unseen force that didn't want him to leave.

When Rand turned around again, the house had changed.

There was an old, box-style television at the front of the living room. It had not been there before. The lamp was on, when seconds before it had been broken. The furniture was completely different from what had been there minutes ago.

It took Rand a few moments to realize what was going on. He was seeing the Swansons' house as it had been in the past.

He was *in* the past.

Finally, the demon's presence had brought Rand to the point in time where the negative spirit was anchored.

Then he heard voices coming from the kitchen.

41

When Kim tried the door again, it opened without resistance. In the front yard, the truck that Carl had arrived in was gone. All the pieces of the event were vanishing, undoing themselves, setting up for the next time the horrific loop would begin again.

Georgia was still there. She waited in the same spot she had been before, palm outstretched, beckoning for them to return.

"Who is that?" Kim asked, wary as she fell behind Stacy's shoulder.

"Relax. She's our way of here."

"How?" Kim asked.

Stacy and Kim crossed the yard. The wind blew mercilessly, whipping Stacy's hair into her face.

"If we touch her, we'll be transported back," Stacy explained.

"Transported where?" Kim asked.

"To reality."

"What—oh, Stacy. Look." Kim pointed behind them toward the house they had just escaped.

Five people stood in a line, watching them go. Bonnie and her two kids and Bonnie's parents. They had a peaceful, light-blue glow surrounding them. The two boys held hands with their mother, one on each side. Even from a distance, Stacy could see the gore that marred their bodies. Bloody holes gaped in their chests and stomachs, left behind from the close-range shotgun blasts.

"They're looking at us," Kim whispered, voice quivering.

"It's okay. We don't need to be afraid of them."

"But what about—"

"That other thing was different. These are friendly."

The family's presence gave Stacy a sense of peace, finally displacing the dread that had filled her all throughout the night.

Kim looked to Georgia and her outstretched hand. "Let's do it before something else weird happens."

"Give me a minute," Stacy said.

Kim glared at her. "For what? We're almost out of here."

Her friend was right. But Stacy remembered something else she had learned from Mr. Casey. These people, brutally killed long before their time, would replay their tragedy over and over, forever.

Unless they're set free.

Stacy crossed the yard again and approached the ghostly family. All five of them kept their gazes on her as she neared. None of them reacted. They only seemed curious about Stacy, as if knowing she didn't belong, but couldn't figure out where she'd come from.

Guiding spirits to the afterlife had been on the second test of the semester. It didn't take much—usually gentle encouragement. Sometimes the spirits just needed permission to forget the evil that kept them anchored to the world of the living.

"There is no need for you to suffer anymore," Stacy said, meeting the eyes of each member of the Erlich family. "I know you all died long before your time. There is a better place waiting for you in the afterlife. You should go there now. There isn't any reason left for you to stay here."

Stacy looked at Bonnie. Although the girl's face was unclear—a common characteristic of a ghostly apparition—Stacy could've sworn the woman was smiling at her.

"If you see the light, go toward it," Stacy instructed. "That's where you belong. That's where you can finally rest."

Each member of the Erlich family looked up into the sky. Stacy followed their gaze, but saw nothing besides the dark, grey clouds rolling by.

Their apparitions lost shape. The five transformed into orbs of blue light, lifted in the air, and rose higher and higher until Stacy could no longer see them.

They can now be at peace, she thought.

Stacy returned to the other side of the yard where Kim stood beside Georgia.

"I feel like I don't even know you anymore," Kim said, shaking her head in amazement.

"Come on." Stacy took her friend's hand and felt Kim squeeze it.

Stacy reached out to clasp Georgia's outstretched palm.

42

Rand followed the voices to the kitchen, where he found two women sitting at a table. A tall candle burned between them.

Rand had experience with witnessing past events. It happened sometimes when dealing with certain ghosts or entities, especially if he went to a location that had been significant to them during their lifetime.

Who are these two ladies? Rand thought.

"It's important for you to do exactly what I say," one woman said to the other. "This isn't a game, and it can be dangerous if we break the rules. Do you understand, Gerry?"

The other woman, whose back was to Rand, nodded.

Rand realized he was witnessing a younger Geraldine. He went closer to the table and looked at her face. It was definitely her, except her hair was darker and there were far fewer wrinkles.

The two women could not see him, and the scene

before him was not real—it had already happened. Rand was a mere spectator.

The other woman paused and glanced at Rand's feet. She blinked twice.

"Do you see something?" Geraldine whispered.

The woman didn't answer at first, but only continued to listen. "I think there's someone here."

She's a medium, Rand realized. This woman could probably feel Rand's distant presence, even though he was visiting from a different time.

Rand was watching a séance.

Oh no, he thought. Things were starting to make a lot more sense.

The woman broke her attention away from where Rand stood. "Okay. Let's begin."

"Will this take long, Helen?" Geraldine asked. "Wayne has no idea what I'm up to, and if he comes home and sees this, he'll be very upset."

"We can't put a time limit on the spiritual world," Helen said.

Geraldine didn't seem to like that answer, but she nodded regardless.

Helen laid her arms over the table, palms up, and Geraldine took Helen's hands.

"Close your eyes," Helen said. Geraldine obeyed.

"We are here tonight to reach out to the two little boys that we recently lost," Helen said. She paused for a few moments. "They were a very important part of Geraldine's life. She saw them as her own children, and they were cruelly taken from her."

Rand only shook his head. It was no accident that he

was seeing this particular moment of the past. Geraldine probably thought that a medium could help her communicate with the two neighbor boys, but instead they'd made contact with the demonic entities that disguised themselves as the children.

If you invite them, they will come. It was the warning he gave repeatedly in his class.

"Johnny and William, if you are here and you are listening, give us a sign."

Geraldine's face clenched up, as if the mere mention of the two boys' name brought her grief.

"We wish to feel your presence once again. Please come to us."

Helen let the silence linger for a long time. Rand gripped the cross in his hands, on edge, waiting for something to happen. He knew that Johnny and William weren't the spirits that eventually answered Helen's call.

"Johnny and William, we are listening. We are here for you. Please come and speak with us. Give us a sign that you are present."

Footsteps came from above. Light and staccato, like running, barefoot children. Rand and Geraldine looked up at the ceiling at the same time.

"Stay focused," Helen told Geraldine, tightening her grip on the other woman's hands—Geraldine had almost broken the circle.

"That's them," Geraldine whispered. "They always liked to play in the upstairs loft when they came over."

The loft, Rand thought, making a mental note.

"That's our sign," Helen said. "They've come. It makes sense for them to arrive in the loft first, since they have a strong memory of that location. But we want them to come down here and speak with us. Give them more time. When they're comfortable, they'll come."

Helen isn't wrong, Rand thought. *But she doesn't realize that the demonic are very good at impersonating what people want to hear.*

"Johnny and William, thank you for giving us a sign of your presence. We hear you upstairs, and we invite you to come down and join us."

The pitter-patter footsteps came again. Soft children's laughter accompanied them.

Rand craned his head toward the ceiling and followed the sounds of the footsteps. He would have to find the stairs and go up there. If what Geraldine said was true and the loft had been significant to the boys when they were alive, that meant the loft was where Rand needed to go.

Rand turned his back on the séance and started walking from the kitchen to the living room. There was no point watching more when the spirits he was hunting were upstairs.

"Oh. There's someone else here. This presence is *very* strong."

Rand turned and immediately spotted Shindael, who stood just over Helen's shoulder. An ice-cold wave flushed through Rand's entire body.

"Who is it?" Geraldine asked.

Helen's eyebrows pressed together and her lips tightened. "Umm... I don't know." She lifted her chin to speak. "New spirit who has joined us... We welcome you. Please identify yourself."

Rand thought he could see an amused smile behind Shindael's small, black eyes.

"Leave them alone," Rand said.

Shindael grasped Helen's shoulder, his thin-fingered hand seeming to crush the woman's petite frame. Helen gasped and shot up from her seat, yanking her hands from Geraldine's.

Shindael vanished.

"What's wrong?" Geraldine asked.

Helen rubbed the shoulder that Shindael had touched. "I have to go." She looked like she was about to cry.

"Helen, wait."

Helen stormed right past Rand, not seeing him or sensing his presence. She scooped up her purse from the coffee table with a trembling hand. "Something feels wrong. I'm sorry." Then she rushed out the door, leaving Geraldine alone and confused.

Once Helen was gone, Geraldine blew out the candle.

They did not close the ceremony properly, Rand thought. Shindael and the two entities that had responded to Helen's call would remain. Rand was honestly surprised it had taken entire decades for the Swansons to start having problems.

Rand crossed the living room and entered another part of the house, which he had not previously seen. Off to the side, he found the stairwell. The darkness seemed to grow thicker with each step up.

Geraldine appeared beside him. She was oblivious to his presence. She also gazed upstairs, seeming confused and intrigued at the same time.

"Don't go," Rand whispered to her. He knew what was going through the woman's head.

Geraldine started climbing, intent on discovering the source of the children's footsteps.

The loft's darkness swallowed Geraldine.

43

Each step creaked underneath Rand's shoe. When he reached the top, the room lit up—Geraldine had turned on a lamp that sat atop a nearby table. The loft above the Swansons' house appeared to be for storage and was filled with boxes and extra furniture. The ceiling slanted and came to its highest point in the center.

Geraldine looked around. Johnny and William were not there.

But something was making those noises, Rand thought. *Something is up here.*

Rand then grew extremely cold. The chill was familiar to him. Something evil was present—something Geraldine could not see.

Geraldine rubbed her palms along her arms, trying to warm up. She must have also felt the unnatural chill in the air. She also looked wary.

It seemed to become too much for Geraldine to bear. She rushed down the stairs, leaving Rand alone in the loft.

Rand surveyed the loft—and found the demon behind him. It was the elder black-eyed kid. He still retained his true, shadowy form. The creature was nestled in the corner of the ceiling.

Rand backed away as icy needles prickled his skin.

He'd said the other kid was with Stacy, Rand thought. *This one has come for me.*

The demon climbed down from the ceiling corner, long legs and arms moving like an insect. His substantial body blocked the top of the stairs, trapping Rand inside the loft.

Rand sensed the wall growing closer behind him. The loft was a small space. Keeping his distance would be impossible. It was going to be a close-quarters fight.

Rand raised the cross and placed it between him and approaching demon. With one swift movement from his clawed hand, the demon swiped at the cross and snapped it in half, leaving Rand holding only a small piece of splintered wood.

Before Rand could fully comprehend what had happened, the demon zipped behind Rand, and wrapped his long arms around Rand's body.

The air was forced from Rand's lungs. His sternum and ribs bent under the demon's strength, and he knew any tighter a squeeze would shatter them. The pressure built in his throat and face, like his head was in danger of popping off.

Rand's instinct took over like a drowning man struggling for the water's surface. He clawed at the arms, but found no relief.

He had never been attacked like this before. This was

far worse than the scratches and beatings he'd endured from other demons.

A new pain bloomed. Rand realized the entity's touch was so cold it burned, like dry ice searing into his skin. He didn't have the breath to scream.

Then Shindael was in front of him, having materialized from thin air.

He was inches away from Rand, watching the man struggle in his servant's grasp.

'You're not praying.' Shindael's words filled Rand's head. *'Perhaps you should start.'*

What was the point? When had it ever helped before?

Shindael smirked. He'd read that thought.

Rand realized he was right where Shindael had always wanted. Trapped, hopeless, and worst of all, faithless.

'It has been my pleasure to torment you, Randolph. But the time has come for us to finish this. You bested Karax. You prevailed over Hazul. You have foiled the plans of my master, the devil, for too long, and now he commands your death.'

Because of the pain, it took Rand a few moments to comprehend what Shindael was saying.

The game was over. The end had come. The long-armed demon had captured Rand so easily and was crushing him to death. Rand had never had a chance.

The edges of his vision blurred and his consciousness began to flicker out. The only thing he saw clearly now was a white light that had appeared behind Shindael.

There it was again. The same white light Rand had seen in the woods. Now he knew he was dying.

Except... he hadn't been dying when he'd seen the light the first time.

This is something else, Rand realized.

With the only remaining air in his lungs, he forced out two words. "Behind you."

The oldest trick in the book.

Shindael turned.

The light started to morph. It took the form of a girl with silver, flowing hair who wore a white dress. Her striking eyes were also completely white.

Shindael roared. It was a deep and powerful sound that Rand had never heard from the demon before. Shindael had always been stoic, but when he saw the girl, his calm demeanor broke.

Shindael was *afraid* of her.

Shindael's apparition dissolved into a cloud of smoke. That cloud vanished from the room in the next instant. He'd fled from the girl.

Rand felt the shadowy arms around him relax. The appearance of the white-eyed girl and the abandonment of the demon's master had caused him to slip.

Rand's mind worked fast. Shindael feared the white-eyed girl. That meant the demon that held him did as well.

Rand twisted out of the demon's loosened grasp and broke free. In the next instant, he grabbed the black arm and pulled. The demon's strength and resolve had left him.

Rand shoved the demon toward the girl. The white-eyed girl lifted her hands, as if to catch the creature. As soon as the two made contact, the demon unleashed a guttural howl.

Then he burst into a splatter of black plasma. The disgusting fluid painted the walls, the floor, and even sprayed onto Rand's clothes.

None of it touched the white-eyed girl.

The spike of adrenaline faded all at once. Rand dropped to his hands and knees, gasping for air to fill his lungs. His bones ached, and the cold burning from the demon's touch had seared through his jacket and shirt and left stinging red marks on his flesh underneath his tattered clothes. His palms burned too, from having grabbed the demon's arms.

Rand looked up. He was at the feet of the girl. She seemed about ten years old, but it was hard to see clearly now. Her light was so radiant Rand found it difficult to look directly at her.

Despite the pain in Rand's body, an overwhelming comfort flowed through him. He felt peace and calm. Somehow, he knew the feelings were coming from the white-eyed girl. He didn't ever want to leave. Tears welled up in his eyes. He felt unworthy to be in her presence.

"Who are you?" Rand managed.

The two pieces of the broken cross that lay on the ground moved by themselves. They zipped over and sealed themselves together at the girl's bare feet, reattaching and mending themselves as if it had never been broken.

'You are a faithful servant.'

Her voice filled Rand's head. It sounded like the most beautiful music he'd ever heard.

'Now go and rest.'

The light that emanated from the girl grew brighter, blinding Rand and forcing him to cover his eyes with his arm. When he could see again, he was somewhere else.

44

R and lay supine, looking up into the starry sky. The cross, now whole, rested on his chest.

He found the strength to push himself onto his elbows and looked around. He was in the front yard of Wayne Swanson's house. A group of people were nearby.

His eyes adjusted, and he spotted Miller, Libby, Wayne, and Geraldine. The group didn't know he was there. They spoke amongst themselves and hadn't yet noticed his sudden reappearance.

"Hey," Rand called out.

All of their heads snapped toward him at once, startled.

"It's Rand!" Miller's voice. The group rushed over.

Miller looped his forearms into Rand's armpits and pulled him to his feet. A wave of dizziness hit him. "Easy, Miller."

The cross tumbled off his chest and landed in a pile of leaves. Libby picked it up.

"How did you get out here?" Miller asked. "We just watched you walk inside the house."

Rand rubbed at his eyes. His fingertips came away wet. The last of the tears were still there. "That's time distortion for you."

"Are you okay, Dad?" Libby asked. "What happened in there?"

"Your clothes are all ripped up," Miller said.

Everyone looked at him expectantly, waiting for his answers. Wayne Swanson still held his shotgun.

"That entity won't be bothering you anymore," Rand told Wayne. "Wait… Stacy. Where's Stacy?"

He was met by grim silence.

If Stacy hadn't returned yet, then surely she was in trouble. *I have to find a way back to the past,* he thought.

There was movement—someone was coming toward them. Everyone turned toward the sound of footsteps crunching through the leaves. Wayne readied his gun.

As they neared, Rand realized it was actually three people approaching. He recognized Stacy first, and she was with a girl dressed in a black leotard. Georgia was behind them, pulling her oxygen tank along.

Rand rushed over to his student. "Are you okay?"

Stacy didn't answer, and instead wrapped him in a tight hug. Rand felt the tension in her body. It eased out of her as they embraced.

"Are *you* okay?" Stacy asked him. "Your clothes are ripped. What happened to you?"

"I had a little standoff with one of the black-eyed kids," Rand said.

"I was with the younger one," Stacy said.

Rand pulled away from Stacy and gripped her shoulders. "And?"

"I beat him. And I got Kim back."

The girl beside Stacy looked haggard and spent, as if she'd just been released from a torture chamber. Rand could only imagine what Kim must have experienced while being held captive.

"I'm sorry you went through this," Rand told Kim. The apology sounded hopelessly hollow to his ears.

Kim couldn't seem to muster the strength to respond. She only leaned against Stacy for support.

Kim's brokenness weighed heavy on Rand. The girl was yet another innocent that had been harmed for the sole purpose of tormenting him.

Wayne Swanson appeared at Rand's side. "This is all very touchin', but it's way past my bedtime. Are you tellin' me that I don't have anythin' to worry about anymore... with those things? They scare my dog."

"Your dog will be happy to know that they're gone," Rand said.

It seemed to take all of Wayne's willpower to force his hand out toward Rand. He shook it. Maybe Rand *was* a paranormal nut, but he was happy to help.

The Swansons returned to their home while shouting at Boss to follow them. The cold dog was more than happy to run back inside.

Georgia held up her hand to Rand, and Rand high-fived her. "Next time I'm going to charge you, Ghost Man."

Rand smirked. "Deal."

"You sure everything's good?" Libby asked.

Rand nodded. "I'm sure. And I'm exhausted. Let's all

go home. Libby, can you take Georgia back to the hospital?"

"Yeah," Libby said. "Come on, Georgia."

"Can I drive this time?" Georgia asked.

"Have you ever driven a car before?" Libby asked.

"Sure. In video games." Libby gave Georgia a look. "Come on, what's the worst that can happen at this point? I crash it?"

"Ugh, I know. Bill's going to freak out when he sees this."

"He can just buy another one, can't he? Isn't he a billionaire?"

The two girls continued talking as they walked toward Bill's half-destroyed BMW. They got in and drove away.

Rand, Miller, Stacy, and Kim returned to Rand's Jeep. The two girls climbed into the backseat.

"Hey." Miller eyed Rand over the Jeep's hood. "What happened in there? To us, you were only gone for a few minutes."

"It was a white-eyed girl," Rand said.

Miller blinked. "A what?"

"Yeah. The demon had me trapped. Shindael was there too. They were just about to kill me. And then she appeared."

"Do you think…"

"I do," Rand said.

Miller's mouth fell open. "That's *huge*. Have you ever seen an angel before?"

"No."

Miller smirked. "I *told* you God hasn't abandoned you."

He sure did wait until the last possible minute, Rand thought. "But that's not all. When I escaped, I threw the demon toward the girl. She touched him, and when she did, he..." He gestured with his hands as he sought the right word. "Exploded."

"Exploded?"

"Yeah. Black plasma went everywhere." He gestured to the black stains on his clothes. "He was just gone, like a popped balloon."

Miller digested that information for a few moments. "This is a big deal, Rando."

"She was an angel and all she had to do was touch the demon. She killed him."

"If you're right, then this is a *huge* breakthrough."

Miller was right. In all his encounters, Rand had only ever been able to send the demonic entities back to hell. They were free to return to Earth whenever they wanted. He'd even encountered some demons more than once.

Never before had he been able to actually *kill* them. That was supposed to be impossible. Demons weren't alive—they were merely spirits. How could you kill something that wasn't technically alive? But demons fled from anything holy for a reason.

Now, Rand had seen that reason with his own two eyes.

That was how Rand was sure that the girl he'd seen was an angel of the Lord.

He was filled with hope. This changed everything. If only the angel had touched Shindael, too. But Shindael had taken off as soon as he'd glimpsed the girl.

"We'll talk more about it later," Rand said. "For now, let's go home."

"Are you in a rush?" Miller asked. "Can we stop for breakfast?"

Rand rolled his eyes.

The first rays of dawn broke. Finally, after the long hours of cold darkness, the world was brightening.

Rand and Miller climbed into the Jeep and Rand started off down Plaster Road. As he drove, the sky became a brighter blue, chasing away the stars until the top of the orange sun peeked over the horizon.

It was approaching eight in the morning by the time Rand got home after dropping off Stacy and Kim, then Miller. The weather radar was still on the television from when he'd rushed out after Stacy had called.

He started walking toward his bedroom but halted when the Bible on the coffee table caught his eye.

Something was different. He approached it slowly, trying to place it.

Then it occurred to him. It was turned to a different page than he'd left it. The previous night, he'd been reading the story of Job. Now, the Bible was open to the very end of the Book of Revelation.

Long ago, Rand had highlighted and underlined a verse in those final chapters.

"And the devil that deceived them was cast into the lake of fire and brimstone, where the beast and the false prophet are, and shall be tormented day and night for ever and ever."

Rand couldn't help but smile.

Lord, Rand prayed, *thank you for revealing your power to me. I know my faith has been fragile, but I am your servant and warrior.*

The prayer was short, but that was okay. It was the most authentic prayer he'd managed in a long, long time.

RAND PACED the front of the classroom as his students busied themselves with their midterm. It was the same test he gave every semester, and it was easy. Certainly the students in the other religion classes were stressing out over their essay tests. Rand's students, however, were soaring through, flipping the pages and circling the obvious answers to the multiple-choice questions.

But Rand's gaze kept returning to the empty desk in the front row—the one usually occupied by Stacy Thompson. He hadn't heard from her at all since he'd dropped her off at home a few nights before.

One by one the students finished and walked to the front to hand in their exams. Rand stacked them. Toward the end of the class, the only person left was Garrett, the lone student in the class who had a failing grade. He scratched at this head as he read and reread the questions, flipping the pages back and forth.

Eventually, Garrett gave up, making his guesses with big, frenzied circles on his paper, then went to the front of the room to turn in his test.

Rand shoved the tests into his bag and slung it over his shoulder. He'd grade them that night. Or maybe give Libby a couple bucks to do it.

He stopped by his office first on the way to the parking lot. There, he had a visitor waiting for him in the hall by his office door.

Stacy sat with her knees up to her chest, arms

wrapped around her legs. She looked very distressed, and she stood as soon as she saw him.

"I was worried about you," Rand said. "Everything okay?"

Stacy shrugged.

Rand unlocked his office and the two went in together. He took his seat behind his desk and Stacy sat in the chair opposite him.

"I'm giving you an A on the test even though you skipped it," Rand said. "After everything that happened, you've earned—"

"I dropped your class."

Rand immediately felt deflated. Within the first few weeks in the semester, anyone could drop a class without repercussions to their GPA. But Stacy would receive a W on her transcript, which stood for "Withdraw." It was worse than an F.

"Why? You didn't have to do that. You should have talked to me first."

"I had to do it, Mr. Casey. I can't spend another minute in your class, absorbing all the stuff you teach. Not after what happened the other night. And if I stay in the class, I know I'll study for it, which means I'll be thinking about the material all the time. I have to drop it. It's better that way."

Rand sighed. They could have worked something out. He would have been happy to have let her never come back and still give her an A.

But he remembered how traumatized Stacy had been on Halloween night. She'd stepped up and saved her friend when it mattered, yet the whole ordeal would leave a lasting scar on her for the rest of her life.

"But what about the easy A?" Rand asked.

Stacy shook her head. "I don't care about my GPA anymore. There are some things that are more important. Like guarding myself from these things that you teach us about."

"I suppose you have a point," Rand said. A brief silence fell between them. "How's your shoulder?"

Stacy stretched the collar of her shirt down to show where the black-eyed kid had grabbed her. The handprint was still visible, but the redness had started to fade.

"Almost gone," Rand said. He could hear the guilt behind his tone. Stacy should have never suffered an injury like that in the first place.

Stacy slung her backpack over her shoulder and stood. "Thank you for being there for me when I needed you. You're the best teacher I've ever had." She held out her hand, and Rand shook it.

Stacy left his office, and just like that, his star student was gone. He collapsed back into his chair and let out a deep sigh. Even when he won, he still lost.

Rand logged into his computer and brought up the presentation he'd given the other day—the lesson on the things he didn't believe in. He navigated to the slide on the black-eyed kids. The picture he'd pasted on the slide had nowhere near the same effect as the kids in real life.

Rand studied the picture for a few seconds. Then he selected the entire slide and pressed the delete key.

The black-eyed kids vanished from the screen.

Randolph Casey will return!

To be notified as soon as he does, visit my website to sign up to my email list.

https://rockwellscott.com/free-book/

As soon as you sign up, you'll also receive a FREE gift from me—my supernatural horror novella that is not available anywhere else. You'll be able to download the book directly to your e-reading device in seconds.

HEY THERE.

Thank you for spending your valuable time reading my book, and I hope you enjoyed it.

As you may know, reviews are one of the best ways readers can support their favorite authors. They help get the word out and convince potential readers to take a chance on me.

I would like to ask that you consider leaving a review on Amazon or Goodreads. I would be very grateful, and of course, it is always valuable to me to hear what my readers think of my work.

Thank you in advance to everyone who chooses to do so, and I hope to see you back in my pages soon.

Sincerely,

- Rockwell

ALSO BY ROCKWELL SCOTT

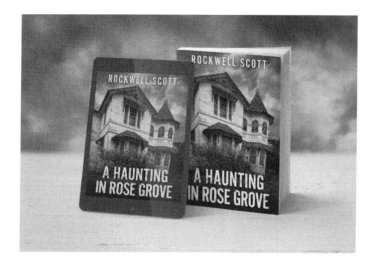

A Haunting in Rose Grove

**A malevolent entity. A violent haunting. A house with a
bloody history. Jake Nolan left it all behind, but now he must
return.**

Jake has it all — a new home, an amazing girlfriend, and nearing
a promotion at work. Best of all, he feels he's finally moved on
from the horrors of his traumatic past. But when he learns that
his estranged brother, Trevor, has moved back into their
haunted childhood home, Jake knows his past is not quite
finished with him yet.

Jake rushes to the old house in Rose Grove — a small town with
a tragic history — to pull his brother from that dangerous place.

But it's too late. There, he finds Trevor trying to make contact with the spirit that tormented them years ago.

And Trevor refuses to leave. He is determined to cleanse the house and remove the entity. But the supernatural activity becomes too much to handle, and Jake knows they are both unprepared for the fight. Worse, the entity targets Daniel, Jake's young nephew, and wants to bring him harm. And when the intelligent haunting shows signs of demonic infestation, Jake realizes they aren't dealing with a mere ghost.

Jake attributes the evil spirit for driving his parents to an early grave. Now it wants to claim the rest of the family, and the only way Jake and Trevor will survive is to send the entity back to hell.

A Haunting in Rose Grove is a supernatural horror novel for readers who love stories about haunted houses and battles with the demonic — the truest form of evil that exists in our world.

ALSO BY ROCKWELL SCOTT

The Gravewatcher

Every night at 3 AM, he visits the graveyard and speaks to someone who isn't there.

Eleanor has created an ideal life for herself in New York City with a career that keeps her too busy, just as she likes it. But when she receives an anonymous message that her estranged brother Dennis is dead, her fast-paced routine grinds to a halt. She rushes to Finnick, Louisiana — the small, backward town where her brother lived and temporarily settles into his creepy, turn-of-the-century house until she can figure out how he died.

But that night, Eleanor spots a young boy in the cemetery behind Dennis's house, speaking to the gravestones. When she approaches him, Eleanor's interruption of the boy's ritual sets off a chain reaction of horror she could have never prepared for. The footsteps, the voices, and the shadowy apparitions are only the beginning.

Eleanor learns that the boy, Walter, is being oppressed by a demonic entity that compels him to visit the graveyard every night. She suspects Dennis also discovered this nightly ritual and tried to stop it, and that is why he died. Because there are others in Finnick who know about Walter's involvement with the evil spirit and want it to continue, and they will do whatever it takes to stop Eleanor from ruining their carefully laid plans. Now Eleanor must finish what her brother started — to rescue the boy from the clutches of hell before he loses his soul forever.

The Gravewatcher is a supernatural horror novel for readers who love stories about haunted houses, creepy graveyards, and battles with the demonic - the truest form of evil that exists in our world.

ABOUT THE AUTHOR

Rockwell Scott is an author of supernatural horror fiction.

When not writing, he can be found working out, enjoying beer and whiskey with friends, and traveling internationally.

Feel free to get in touch!

Facebook
www.facebook.com/rockwellscottauthor

Twitter
@rockwell_scott

www.rockwellscott.com

rockwellscottauthor@gmail.com

Printed in Great Britain
by Amazon

50866037R00173